MAGIC CRIES

ECHOES BOOK TWO

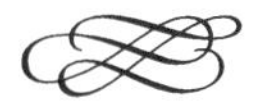

MIRIAM GREYSTONE

* * *

Be sure to join my Insiders list to get free sneak peeks, new release notices, and giveaways! Join here: http://www.miriamgreystone.com/connect-with-me/

Molly's story begins in Magic Calls . . .

Available now on Amazon!!
http://www.miriamgreystone.com/getbook1

For Yocheved

"Friendship . . . is born at the moment when one man says to another 'What! You too? I thought that no one but myself . . .'"

- C.S. Lewis

“the moon understands dark places.
the moon has secrets of her own.
she holds what light she can.”
- Lucille Clifton

Moonchild

MOLLY

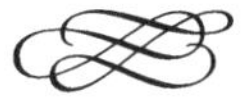

The metro hurtled by, sleek, silver, and deadly. Molly pressed her cheek against the tunnel wall, her fingernails scraping against the grime-caked stone, and held her breath as the train thundered past. Air pressure slammed against her, the train so close that she could have touched it with the tips of her fingers. Somehow, the idea of closing her eyes made it worse, so she watched as the lights and metal screamed by, her hair whipping in her face, the blood pounding in her ears.

"When I said that I would help you," she yelled hoarsely in Matt and Thia's direction, "I had no idea that this kind of near-death experience would be involved!"

"You're perfectly safe!" Matt hollered back, though the fact that he had his eyes squeezed shut and his face pressed tightly against the filthy concrete made his words less than reassuring. "These ledges are built so that metro workers can take shelter if they're accidentally in the wrong place and a train comes by! You'll be fine!"

"If Lena is an Echo," Molly yelled back over the train's chaotic din, "why would she live in a place that you can only access by going through here?"

"Because she fucking hates us!" Matt shouted, smiling broadly with his eyes still closed.

The last car clattered thunderously as it passed, and then the train was gone.

For a second, no one moved. Molly pushed away from the wall, wishing her legs didn't feel so damn shaky. Bits of grit and dirt clung to the side of her face and her palms. She looked down at her watch glowing dimly in the darkness. They only had about six minutes before the next train came.

Matt came to stand beside her, looking a bit wobbly himself. The entire back of his shirt and pants were black with soot and filth.

Thia, who had been a few feet further down the tunnel, uncurled from the crevice where she had wedged herself.

"Lena likes solitude," she told Molly, as she tried to brush a little of the soot from her shirt. Mostly her efforts just distributed the grime more evenly. Some of her long blonde hair had escaped from its ponytail, and she pushed it hurriedly back behind her ears. "She and the old guy she calls her teacher live in the most remote parts of the tunnel system. It's their not-so-subtle way of telling us they don't like visitors."

"One has to wonder what exactly that guy is 'teaching' her," Matt muttered as he began to pick his way over the track.

Thia laughed as she followed him, though it sounded a little forced. "Knock it off, Matt, you know that's ridiculous. People say that he's the oldest living Echo. He's way too old for her."

"People say a lot of things," Matt grunted, as he checked the battered map he clutched in his hand. "It doesn't make them true. Come on," he encouraged them, his voice unbearably chipper, "if the map is right, then we've got just enough time to make it through the opening before the next train comes by."

That was enough to motivate all three of them, and they ran as fast as the semi-darkness and uneven ground under their feet would allow. Molly asked herself for the one-thousandth time why she had agreed to come along on this . . . what was it, anyway? A mission? An excursion? A passive-aggressive death wish expressed by snuggling up with one hundred-ton trains traveling at fifty miles per hour?

"Remind me why am I doing this?" she said, asking the question out loud when she found that she really couldn't answer it herself. "Because I'm questioning all of my life choices right now."

"You're here because we need you," Matt grinned, glancing over his shoulder toward her as he ran. "Lena probably won't talk to me or Thia, and she definitely wouldn't talk to Andrew. But you're a fresh face. A new person who she won't spit at on sight. Which makes your presence super helpful."

"Here it is," Thia interrupted them, stopping in the center of the track and kneeling down next to what looked like a round sewer cover emblazoned with the metro logo. Immediately businesslike, Matt pulled out the crowbar that he had strapped to his back and bent down to help her pry the cover off.

Molly stood behind them, shifting her weight from one foot to the other and glancing over her shoulder every other second. She hated the idea of hugging the tunnel wall as another train rushed past. But being caught standing squarely in the center of the tunnel when the train arrived would definitely be worse. "Maybe we should wait till after the next train goes by?" she suggested reluctantly after rechecking her watch.

"Too late," Matt grunted without looking back at her. He had managed to pry the round, iron cover part way off. His shoulders strained with effort. "Can't have the cover half off when the train passes. Might cause it to derail. At this point, we're all-in."

"Shit," Molly responded, her heart rate picking up even more. "How can I help?"

"Lift . . . here . . ." Thia groaned, and Molly hurried to join them, wrapping her fingers around the cover's rough edges, and pulling as hard as she could. Together, the three of them slid the heavy cover to the side, revealing the opening beneath it. Molly peered down and saw nothing but blackness.

"We're sure this is the right place?" Molly breathed, trying not to imagine what would happen if she jumped into the pitch-black shaft and it wasn't the entryway Andrew had promised. How accurate could his maps even *be*? He'd been evasive when she asked where he had gotten them. And what else might be down there in the dark that Andrew didn't know about?

"No time for second guessing now!" Matt announced, the cheerfulness in his voice so forced that it grated on Molly's ears. "The next train is coming. Everybody in!" Molly could feel the vibrations in the ground mounting as the train got closer. She hesitated, looking down into the hole, trying to see something . . . anything . . . through the blackness. But the gloom was too thick, and there were no other options.

She paused just long enough to glare at Matt, "If I die doing this I will absolutely kill you," she hissed at him. Then, one foot after the other, she lowered herself into the darkness, and let herself fall.

She rolled as soon as she hit the bottom, feeling the air rush out of her on impact. She heard Matt and Thia drop just seconds later, softly cursing as they landed. Weak, mottled, yellow light streamed through the opening above them, and Molly stumbled back toward it on unsteady feet to help Matt and Thia tug the iron cover back into place.

No one spoke as they worked, all three of them straining furiously as the noise of the train's approach got closer and closer. Molly's arms burned, her breath coming in quick, desperate gasps. It wasn't so much that the cover was too heavy to move, but it was hard to get a good enough hold on it to be able to pull it back into place. Molly had to stand on her tiptoes just to reach it. Finally, the iron disk gave in, settling into its place with a harsh grating sound.

The train roared above their heads. They stood, breathing heavily, silent and blind in the darkness, and listened to it pass.

Unlike the metro tunnel, there were no emergency lights here to break up the blackness. When the train above them had passed, Thia pulled a flashlight from her pocket and switched it on.

"Holy shit," she gasped, rotating so the light panned across the tunnel walls. "Looks like we found the right place."

Molly had seen some of Lena's paintings before. On the night that they had fled from Steele's invasion of the Refuge, they had passed some artwork, plastered on the deserted tunnel walls. But still, she wasn't prepared for what she was looking at now.

The images were painted right onto the wall in colors so bright that Molly was surprised they hadn't shined through the darkness. Lena's other paintings had been haunting, but these were more intimate. Raw, somehow. As though Lena had never intended any eyes but her own to see them. As though the paintings were the diary of a deeply disturbed mind, left with the pages open, staring at them from every inch of those walls.

A hundred faces, contorted with pain and sorrow, mouths screaming with no sound, stared out at them. Their gazes seemed to ask Molly a hundred questions she could never hope to answer. Grasping hands, bloody fingers, painted with so much detail and raw talent that they seemed ready to break through the cement and catch hold of Molly's arm as she passed. Even the tunnel's ceiling was covered with the images of at least a dozen moons, painted wide and white and somehow mournful. At the very center of the wall was a painting of a man, standing with his face upturned toward those moons, a knife clasped in his fist, his hands and arms soaked and dripping with blood. He reached toward the sky in heartbroken supplication.

They stared, speechless. For once, even Matt didn't have anything funny to say. Then, still silent, they began to walk slowly down the tunnel. There were more images, crowded together, sometimes one on top of the other, covering every inch of the tunnel wall from ceiling to floor. Lena had painted hundreds of eyes, all wide and staring, that seemed to watch them as they passed. Images of children, drawn with round, wailing mouths, their hands lifted as though to press against the wall, as if they were somehow trapped on the other side. Near the ceiling, huge black birds with curved beaks and featherless heads were circling, locked in an endless search for carrion.

"You said that Andrew found Lena in a psych ward?" Molly asked in a whisper.

"That's right," Thia nodded. "He used his voice to convince the doctors to let him walk her right out. He brought her back to the Refuge with him, but she disappeared into the tunnels after just a few days."

"It's strange," Matt added in an undertone. "Why does she hate him so much if he's the one who got her out of there?"

The beam of Thia's flashlight reached a new patch of tunnel wall, and Molly's feet froze.

"Might make sense, actually," Molly whispered hoarsely, "if the hospital was where she needed to be."

Images of countless bodies lying motionless on a beach, moonlight streaming down on them as a light rain fell. Hundreds of feathers floated in the air. The sand ran red with blood.

For a long moment, none of them spoke.

"We'd better keep moving," Molly said at last, and Matt and Thia both shook themselves and nodded in agreement. They moved carefully in the darkness. The tunnel sloped downward, and it was hard not to slip. Molly's eyes kept drawing back to the walls. The murals changed as they moved further down the passage, each image more troubling and haunting than the last. After a few minutes of walking, she saw most of the paintings they were passing now were obscured by thick black letters. "THIS ISN'T RIGHT," Lena had written over and over again, until the pictures were almost obliterated by her angry scrawl, with only a flash of color or a single, staring eye visible at the margins of the words. In another place, she had written the word "NO" at least a hundred times with a dark red substance that Molly sincerely hoped was paint.

"How much farther is it?" Molly asked, not realizing until she spoke that her voice had dropped to a whisper.

Matt's response seemed unnaturally loud, his voice jarring in the gloom. "There's no way to really know," he told her, glancing down at the crumpled map in his hand. "No one's seen her for at least six months. We used to catch glimpses of her pretty regularly in the tunnels, and sometimes she would just show up in the Refuge. She'd come and sit in the Tavern—not eating, but just watching the people. It creeped a lot of people out, honestly. But then she stopped coming. People thought that maybe her 'training' got too intensive." Matt raised his eyebrows suggestively, but Molly could tell that his heart wasn't in the joke. He was just trying to break up the weight of the darkness that seemed to grow heavier on their shoulders with every step.

"It just got too hard for me," a low voice answered. Molly spun to face the sound.

Lena held a small jar in her hand that glowed and bathed her face in green and yellow light. Slight and so short that her head wouldn't have come up even to Molly's shoulder, she stood just off to the right of them, in front of a curved, metal doorway they had walked right past but hadn't even seen. Her lips curved upward into a smile so tentative it looked like it pained her. Her skin was pale and seemed to almost glow in the darkness. She wore her black, thickly curled hair parted in the middle; it hung down past her shoulders, some of it braided in the front to keep it out of her eyes. The loose-fitting sweatshirt she wore seemed to practically swallow her up, and where the sleeves were pushed up from her wrists, Molly could see that both of her arms were covered in a complicated tangle of black tattoos. Her fingers were stained with every color of paint, it was sunk deep into her skin and caked under her fingernails. Her stature was so slight that Molly might have guessed her to be no more than fifteen or sixteen years old if it hadn't been for her eyes.

Her eyes looked older.

The girl stepped closer, dirty bare feet visible beneath her tattered jeans.

"I wanted to come," she told them, as though they were in the middle of a long conversation, "and Malcolm said that it was better for me to be with people. At least sometimes. But it hurt too much. People smiled at me. But all I could see was corpses with dead eyes staring."

For a second they all just stared. Matt's mouth hung open a little, and Molly could see him struggling to figure out how on earth to respond to that.

"We understand," he stammered at last, though Molly could see clearly he didn't. She saw Lena's eyes narrow a little, as though she had also heard the lie that bordered on condescension in his voice. "We don't mean to bother you. We just have a few questions to ask you, and then we'll go away and leave you to your important work." Matt didn't really think her painting was important, and he sounded like he was talking to a child.

Lena took a small step back.

"What questions do you have?" she asked, her eyes turning to Thia. "I remember you," she tilted her head a little. "You're the one who swam in the darkness until it washed the worst parts of her memories away. Have they resurfaced yet?" Lena asked. "Or can you still not remember?"

Thia's eyes were as round as saucers. She tried to respond, but at first, no sound came out. She swallowed hard and tried again. "I . . . I still don't remember most of it," she admitted, her tone one of mild surprise. "But I think it's for the best, really. Those memories weren't doing anything but ripping me apart inside. And it's all over anyway. What good would thinking about it do?"

Lena frowned and looked down thoughtfully at the glowing jar she grasped in her hands. "Unseen is not the same as gone. Sometimes threats are greatest when they swim beneath the surface of our sight. When we feel pain, we know we are sick, and we need treatment. But if we silence the pain, while the sickness still grows, how can we know what ails us? And how can we ever hope to heal?"

Thia had gone white while Lena spoke. Molly was used to Thia's easy smile, the teasing light in her eyes, the laughter that always seemed so eager to bubble to her lips. There was no laughter in her now.

"I don't want to remember," Thia said at last, her voice a whisper that Molly had to strain to hear. "I couldn't bear it. I'm not ready."

Lena nodded deeply. "When the time is right then," she agreed and turned her eyes toward Molly.

"I don't know you," she commented, and stepped closer to Molly, staring at her intently. Lena's laser-sharp gaze ran over her. She studied the brown and red streaked thick hair hanging down to Molly's shoulders, and the black short sleeve shirt, stained with soot, that she wore. Her eyes ran over the thick bracelets Molly wore on her wrist and upper arm, the skeleton key tattoo on her shoulder. Molly felt naked, as though Lena could see through her, could see the scars on her arms that her bracelets and tattoos hid, and even deeper, to the scars inside of her that she had never willingly shown to any living soul.

"What questions?" Lena asked again, but this time, she was asking Molly.

Molly fidgeted with one of her bracelets, finding the feel of it on her fingertips reassuring. "We were told that you knew the old songs," she explained, surprised by how uncertain her own voice sounded. What was it about this woman that had shaken her so deeply? "Ballads you learned from your teacher about the history of the Echoes. Stories and legends that everyone else has forgotten. We were hoping you could tell them to us. They may have information we need."

The corners of Lena's eyes crinkled in an incredulous smile. "None of you have ever wanted to hear my songs," she laughed, and for a second she truly looked like the young girl Molly had almost mistaken her for. "Why do you want to listen to them now?"

"Something happened," Molly admitted, feeling as though each word she chose was another step deeper into a minefield she didn't understand. Lena stood light on the balls of her feet, like a deer with its ears pricked up, on the verge of taking flight. "The Refuge was discovered and attacked. There is a man named Steele . . ."

"I know him," Lena said flatly, her face suddenly serious.

Molly nodded, not entirely surprised. "He convinced one of the Echoes to turn traitor and bring him into our hiding place," Molly swallowed. "He killed over twenty Echoes that night and would have killed more of us—all of us—if he could have. Some of us forced him out, and most made it through alive. But our home isn't a secret anymore. Steele knows where we are, and he's more powerful than any of us. He has resources, he has the support of all the Legacies who follow him. If we are going to have any hope of surviving him, we need to be stronger. We need to be able to fight."

Lena's eyebrows pulled together, her brow furrowing. "You think Malcolm's old songs will help you do that?"

"Maybe," Molly answered with a shrug. "Andrew has a plan. There are legends of a goblet that makes the voice of any Echo who drinks from it incredibly powerful. More powerful, even, than Steele. He thinks he knows where the goblet is, now. But it's supposed to be hidden away. Guarded. He thought there might be something in the old songs about it. Something that would help him know how to get to it. What to expect."

Lena's face hardened. Her eyes turned cold, as though a light had been snuffed out inside her. "So, you are here for Andrew?"

"Not just for him," Molly hurried to explain, as Matt and Thia shot panicked looks at each other. Clearly, mentioning Andrew by name had been a mistake. "For all of us."

"I heard what you said before," Lena went on, as though Molly hadn't spoken. "That I hated Andrew for taking me out of the hospital. But you were wrong. I'm not angry at Andrew for taking me out; my fate was never in that place. The doctors there – some of them were kind, and some of them were vultures. None of them could help me. Andrew wasn't bad for taking me out. But he took me to be an instrument played by his hand only. I am a student, and I am young. But I am *not* a pawn. The man who tries to make me into one will come to regret it." She took a step back toward the darkness, and the shadows slid over her face, obscuring her eyes. "I don't help Andrew," she said, her voice ringing with anger. "Not now. Not ever."

She turned, her braided hair flying over her shoulder, her back to them as she started to walk away.

Molly turned to look at Matt and Thia, who stared helplessly back at her. "Do something!" Matt mouthed silently, gesturing urgently with his hands.

Molly ran after her.

"Lena, wait!" she called. She reached out and, with a feather-light touch, lay a hand on Lena's shoulder.

Lena's body went rigid.

She froze in place, her shoulders hunching forward, away from Molly's fingers. Her head snapped back, and eyes that were suddenly dilated and unfocused stared up into the air. Her mouth opened and shut silently, like a fish twisting in a fisherman's net.

"What's wrong with her?" Molly cried, staring at Lena. Frozen in shock.

A strong hand grabbed her shoulder and shoved her aside.

"Alright, which one of you idiots touched her?" a gruff voice demanded. Knocked off balance, Molly stumbled, barely managing to stay on her feet.

"Lena?" the old man said anxiously, moving so that he stood directly in front of her. He didn't touch her, but crouched with his hands on his knees, so that his face was directly across from hers. "Snap out of it, dammit. Pull back. I'm right here, and I'm telling you not to do this right now."

His wide forehead was creased with wrinkles. Thick gray eyebrows gathered like clouds above eyes as black as a gathering storm. His face was a study in valleys and ridges, everything rough, hardened, and worn by age. His thin, colorless lips pressed tight with displeasure as he stared into Lena's face.

"Come on back to me, child," he whispered. "You don't have to be alone in the dark."

Lena blinked. Her fingers uncurled from the tight fists that had formed at her side.

"Malcolm?" she whispered, blinking rapidly, like someone waking from a terrible dream.

"There you go," the old man grunted approvingly. "Come on back now. Easy does it. You'll be alright in just a minute. Just breathe."

Lena gasped and shuddered. Her legs buckled, and she crumpled to the ground.

Matt darted forward, reaching out his arms to support her. Malcolm straightened and shoved Matt away so hard that he fell back several paces.

"What's the matter with you?" he roared. "Are you as stupid as you look? Do you want to send her right into a seizure? She can't bear to be touched. Try to lay a hand on her again, and I'll break every one of your fingers."

"Sorry," Matt held his hands up and backed away. "I didn't know."

"Course you didn't," Malcolm ran a hand through the frizzled gray hair that rose like steam from his scalp. "You haven't got the sense God gave a goose. If you didn't have a map, you probably couldn't find your ass with both hands. Just give the girl some space."

Molly looked down. Lena was clutching her face with her hands. Her hair fell like a black curtain around her, and her shoulders shook.

Malcolm crouched on the ground in front of her, taking care not to touch her.

"Listen to me, Lena. Listen!" he whispered hoarsely, "Whatever you saw . . . wherever it took you . . . the darkness does not own you. You own *it*. You ride its waves. You watch, and you listen, and then you pull away and come back into the light. You don't have to be afraid of it. One day, it'll answer your call like a hound dog coming to heel."

Lena looked up at her teacher through the veil of her hair. Her eyes shone. "Maybe," she shook her head doubtfully. "You keep telling me that. But I'm not there yet."

"Well then, that's why you've got me." For the first time, Malcolm's lips bent into a crooked smile. "You wouldn't want to make a geezer like me feel useless in his old age, would you?"

Lena gave a watery laugh.

"That's my girl. Now. You tell me. What are you?"

Lena pushed her hair out of her face.

"Come on now, don't pretend you don't know it. What are you?"

Lena sighed. "A fighter," she answered, with a roll of her eyes. But the words seemed to steady her a little.

"Damn straight," he murmured, his brow crinkling, and the corners of his mouth lifting in a lopsided grin. "Go on," he whispered, "say the rest. You know you want to."

Lena laughed. She closed her eyes and took a deep breath. When she looked back up at her teacher, her eyes were shining. "I'm a badass bitch with an axe to grind," she recited with a smile.

Her teacher chuckled and slapped his knee. "That's my girl," he crowed. "Those bastards will never know what hit 'em. Right back up again, now." He motioned impatiently, and Lena nodded and rose to her feet.

"Now, I'll ask the three of you again," the old man rotated around slowly and faced them, glaring at each of them in turn. "Which one of you is the idiot that touched her?"

"I did," Molly answered. Malcolm had positioned himself between her and Lena, so Molly had to crane her head to the side in order to meet Lena's eyes. "I'm sorry. I didn't mean for . . . whatever that was . . . to happen. I didn't know."

"It's okay," Lena shrugged. "I mean, it isn't the kind of thing that I'll ever get used to, really. But I know how to get out of it now, at least. And it wasn't your fault."

Molly wondered what Lena had been seeing as she stared up at nothing with a look of horror on her face. What was it about her touch that had such an affect and could cause Lena such distress? But she had a feeling the question wouldn't be welcome.

She also had the feeling that she really might not want to know.

"Who are you?" Malcolm asked her, his eyes narrowing. "And why did you come barging down here in the first place? We've made it as clear as we possibly can that we don't want visitors."

"I'm Molly, and we really didn't mean to bother you," she explained earnestly. "We just wanted information that might help us fight Steele."

"Oh, yes. Steele." The old man shook his head. "That little bastard. I imagine that, once again, he's been making the world an even more miserable place than it already is. Hasn't he?"

"He killed more than twenty Echoes the night he found the Refuge," Thia explained, coming to stand at Molly's shoulder.

Malcolm grimaced. "Aye. No big surprise there. That boy is about as evil as they come."

"That's why we've got to stop him," Molly said eagerly. "I'm pretty new to all of this, to be honest. But I saw what Steele is.

And I know that people like him don't stop hurting others unless someone stands up and *makes* them stop."

Malcolm snorted derisively. "Standing *against* something evil is easy," he said with a dismissive flick of his hand. "Finding what you ought to stand *for*—that's hard. That's where the well-intentioned fools all stumble." He gazed at Molly intently and then gave a shake of his head. "You don't look like a fool, though," he admitted grudgingly.

Molly gave a small smile. "I try very hard not to be."

"Either way, it don't make much difference," Malcolm shoved his hands deep into the pockets of his jeans and rocked back on his heel. "Andrew's going after the goblet, isn't he?" he leaned forward and stared at Molly hard. She nodded.

"Ach, I'm too old for this shit." Malcolm groaned. He turned his head to the side and spat onto the ground. "Listen up." He wiped his mouth with the back of his sleeve. "I'd no more help Andrew get his meaty fingers on that cup than I'd give a toddler a shotgun and then tell 'em to run along and go play in the backyard. You are in way over your head." He lifted his eyes to glare at Matt and Thia. "All of you. And if you don't know that already, you'll learn it soon enough. Lena and I'll have nothing to do with." He turned his head to gaze at Lena. "You ready to go then?" he asked her.

"Almost," she whispered, stepping forward, her eyes focused on Molly.

"You have a tattoo of a key on your arm," Lena observed.

Molly started. Tyler had said something about a key while he was doing his best to kill her. She had been trying very hard not to think about it.

Lena's eyes unfocused a little.

"The man who holds a key in hand thinks himself powerful," she said, her voice a little distant. Molly felt a shiver curl around her spine, "he forgets; it is the key that decides if the lock will slide open, or seal shut." Her eyes snapped back into focus. "Your choices are your own," she told Molly, a fierce edge of anger in her voice. "And you are the one who must live with the consequences. Choose carefully. Because whether you turn to the right or the left, there will be no turning back. Once you pick your path, you will walk that road for the rest of your days."

There was a beat of silence. Everyone stared at Lena, except for her teacher. He stood, his hands still shoved in his pockets, and stared down at his workmen's boots, a solemn expression on his face.

After a minute, he looked up.

"You've said your piece?" he asked Lena, who looked over her shoulder at him and nodded. "Then we're done here." Together, he and Lena began to walk farther down into the tunnel.

"I'm sure you can find your way out!" he yelled to them as they went, not bothering to look back.

Molly, Thia, and Matt stood and watched them go. Molly felt as though she had just received a powerful sucker punch right to her gut.

"I honestly have no idea what just happened," Matt said, shaking his head, his eyes wide and fastened on the patch of darkness that seemed to have swallowed Lena and her teacher.

"We got turned down, that's what," Thia answered.

"It isn't just that, though," Matt protested, holding up his hands. "I mean, I'm not fully human. I'm descended from the Sirens for shit's sake. I can take people's free will away from them with just the sound of my voice. And even *I* thought that was freaky."

"Lena's an Echo, right?" Molly asked.

"Yes," Thia shrugged, "but I have a feeling that isn't *all* she is."

"Well, whatever she is or isn't, this whole day has totally sucked." Matt took the flashlight from Thia's hand and shined it onto the map he was holding, squinting at it resentfully, as though it was making his life difficult on purpose. "And now we have to go back and tell our fearless leader that we couldn't get him what he wanted. I'm sure *that's* going to be a totally enjoyable conversation." He grimaced. "Come on. I think there may be another way out of here. One that, you know, involves less likelihood of death-by-metro."

"Well, that's something, at least." Molly sighed and turned to follow Matt down the tunnel and deeper into the darkness.

JAKE

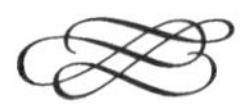

"Come on," Jake felt the mattress shift as Molly sat down beside him. She lay a warm hand on his shoulder. "Wake up?"

Jake didn't open his eyes. He just moved so that he curled around her, and wrapped his arm around her waist. He turned his face away, hoping she wouldn't see the sweat that covered his brow, or notice how fast and uneven his breathing was.

The dream was still pulsing inside him, more real than the world he was waking to.

He had been so happy in the dream.

The pinch of the needle had been so welcome as it settled into his skin, the scratch to a burning itch that tormented him every waking minute of the day. Then he had felt it: the familiar burn that inched through his body, the way his mind went blank and his muscles unclenched. His head fell back as his breathing slowed. His mind flew free. He was in a place with no pain, no regret, no need to worry about the future. Just miles and miles of blue sky. He could fly here forever. Perfect ecstasy.

Then the dream broke and flew from his fingers like water from a shattered glass. Reality crashed back down on him.

Now he felt like throwing up.

He was still clean. It came back to him in a blinding wave of remembered reality. He blinked back tears, pressing his face against the pillow so Molly wouldn't see them. He didn't know if they were tears of relief or unbearable frustration.

He felt so empty. He needed her.

He pressed close against her body, breathing deeply, pulling the smell of her deep inside him, like cleansing incense into a defiled temple. He never had dreams like that when she slept beside him. If only he could be with her all the time, hooked to her, like she was an IV, pumping life-giving sanity into a tainted system that still seemed bent on self-destruction.

He forced himself to sit up, swinging his feet onto the floor and leaning his face into his hands.

"Are you okay?" Molly asked, her voice anxious. Her hand flitted against the wounds on his back. He knew she wanted to check them to see how they were healing, but she was afraid of hurting him.

"Yeah," he muttered into his hands, his voice as rough as gravel, "just sore." He was glad of the injuries now. They had made it so much easier to hide the truth from her. He rubbed his face roughly to make sure his cheeks were dry, digging his knuckles deep into his eyes, glad when it hurt. He was so fucking sick of himself. He wanted his hands to sprout claws and rip his own flesh from his body, searching way down deep to the core of himself, trying to find something, anything, that was pure.

Something that was worthy of sitting next to Molly, and of having her look at him with so much love in her eyes.

He looked back at her, and it hit him, just like always. She was so, so beautiful. All of her was beautiful, the hair that hung down past her shoulders, the eyes the glittered in the semi-dark of their room. The voice, that fell like dew from her lips, so ensnaring that he felt almost sure he could wake from death itself if she called out to him. And most beautiful was her heart. A heart so generous and forgiving that she could look at him—*him*—as broken and tarnished as he was, and think that she saw someone worth loving.

Jake loved her for being wrong about him. Loved her for her ability to see something inside of him that no one—least of all himself—had ever seen before. But he never forgot what he really was. He reached over and wrapped his fingers through hers and held on tight.

He was a disease, bound at any moment to infect the world around him. A ticking time bomb, doomed sooner or later to explode in a haze of destruction and pain. How much longer would he get to be close to her like this? How many days, or hours, or even minutes could he possibly have left before she realized her mistake?

Molly thought that her voice had cured his addiction. She thought it was that simple: she could tell him not to feel the need, and the magic living inside her could sweep his sickness away. Jake knew how deeply wrong she was, but he let her believe it.

It was such a beautiful lie.

He wished, with every ounce of his being that it was true; that he was somehow, miraculously, whole again. Knowing he wasn't, he wished with equal fervor that he had never been born. Soon, any minute now, she would realize how broken he really was; how contaminated and uncurable.

The thought of it made Jake's insides turn to ice, made his lungs clamp down and refuse to take in air. He knew just what would happen once she knew the truth. He could already hear the words somewhere in his head, the familiar echo of words he'd heard before.

"I care about you, Jake. I really do. But you can't be a part of my life unless you're clean. Totally clean. I don't want a junkie." He could hear the sound of the door clicking as it slammed shut. He could feel himself, cold and alone, out on the doorstep.

Everyone else who he thought had loved him had done the

same thing—the right thing. They'd cut and run. Jake had never blamed them for it. And he knew that when Molly saw the truth, she would have to do the same.

This brief time that he had with her—this was more of a dream than the fever-dream of drugs he had just woken from. Jake understood that, with a sudden flash of pain that seared all the way to his core. Being with Molly was a dream he wouldn't get to keep much longer. And when this dream ended, the drugs would be waiting for him like a coyote patiently stalking wounded prey, waiting for the crippled creature to collapse under the weight of its own dysfunction, and then jerk lamely on the ground while it was eaten alive.

"What happened?" Jake asked, forcing the words out, coughing to clear his throat. Molly's face was dirty, and the front of her tee shirt was covered with soot.

Her face hardened. "Well. I didn't die. That's the best thing I can say about my day so far. And seriously, the not-dying part didn't come easy."

"Shit." Jake grabbed Molly's hand, wanting to feel that she was alright. "You've got to be kidding me! I thought you were just going to talk to the woman who did all those paintings. What was her name? Laura?"

"Lena. And that's what we did, more or less. But it was a lot more complicated than anybody told me. Lena wouldn't tell us anything more about how to get to the goblet. She said a lot of other weird stuff though." Molly shuddered as though there were things she'd rather not remember. "I can tell you all about it later," she assured him, seeing the unspoken question in his eyes. "Right now, I have to go find Andrew and let him know we hit another dead end." Molly stood and stretched, grimacing as she arched her back, then pulled open one of the drawers of the dresser that was the one piece of furniture, other than the bed, their room contained, and took out a clean shirt. "He isn't going to be happy."

She peeled off her dirty shirt, throwing it into the corner

before slipping on a new one. The heat in Jake's body soared. Pulled like a magnet across the room toward her, he stood behind her and ran his hands across the warm, smooth plane of her belly.

"Are you sure you have to go?" he whispered, dipping his head and pressing his lips to her ear. "I could probably keep you busy with something else for a while."

Molly laughed and melted into him, letting her head fall back onto his shoulder. She fit perfectly against him. Jake's heart sped up. Being with Molly was the only thing in his whole life that had ever felt better than a high.

"Hmmm. That does sound like a lot more fun than talking to Andrew," she admitted, her voice a little husky. She turned her face toward him and trailed a slow line of kisses from his ear down to his collarbone. "But the sooner I go tell him the bad news, the sooner I can come back."

"Wait," Jake shook off the tingling feel of her skin against his fingers and focused on her words. "Why aren't Matt and Thia going with you?"

"It's almost the second rush." Molly pointed at the ceiling and, sure enough, Jake could hear the distant rumble of metro cars far overhead that signaled the beginning of the afternoon rush hour. "It's almost time to serve lunch, and they've got to get straight to the Tavern and get the food ready before the crowds show up. I told them I'd go update Andrew on my own."

"Sounds like they're ducking out so they don't have to be there when Andrew blows his top," Jake observed, not trying to hide the heat that crept into his voice.

Molly shrugged. "I told them I don't mind. Andrew can be a jerk sometimes, but I'm not afraid of him."

And that, Jake thought to himself, *is exactly the problem.*

Worry twisted in his gut. He knew that Andrew had never been anything but kind to Molly. But Molly had always been useful to Andrew. Jake didn't know the details, but he knew there was something unique about Molly's voice. Something that

Andrew was convinced he would need to get access to the goblet that he was so obsessed with.

Jake couldn't help but worry how things might change if Andrew decided he didn't need Molly anymore.

"I don't like the idea of you going alone," he told her. "I'll come."

"Are you sure?" Molly turned to look at him more closely. "You haven't wanted to go anywhere in a while. Not with your back hurting so much."

"I'll be fine," Jake looked away, running a hand over the bristle of his too-long buzz cut. He had let Molly believe his injuries were keeping him in bed, rather than the dread of halls filled with sounds and scents and people that his drug-deprived system couldn't start to cope with right now. "I don't want you to be by yourself."

He wasn't making any sense, and he knew it. Andrew was the head of the whole Echo community. His voice was more powerful than any of the other Echoes—even Molly, who was fast rising in the ranks and looked to soon become his second in command. And even the *least* powerful of the Echoes could have had Jake on his knees in a split second, with a single command. He had no defenses against them. If Andrew turned on Molly, it wasn't like Jake could do anything to protect her.

But he still wanted to be by her side.

"Sure, come with me." Molly's face lit up. Jake knew that his insistence to stay in their room, in bed, almost constantly, had been worrying her. He'd also been worrying himself. Now she smiled broadly as she watched Jake pull on his shoes. "Maybe we can stop by the Tavern afterward and get something to eat?" Molly added, her voice tentative.

Jake shrugged. "Maybe."

Molly didn't push, for which he was grateful.

Jake looked down at himself. He had been sleeping in a black tee shirt and black jeans; the only kind of clothes he had, ever since he fell down the rabbit hole and into this strange world. Jake didn't mind. The clothes the Echoes had provided to him were far nicer than anything he would have owned. The clothes were a bit rumpled, but there was no point in changing; he would look like shit no matter what he wore. The wounds on his back from Tyler's beating were mostly healed over, but the deep bruises on his face were taking a long time to fade. Somehow, the longer they took to heal, the worse they looked, changing from swollen pink and gray to deep, bright shades of blue and purple.

His right hand, which he had thrust deep into a fire on the first night he had been dragged down into the tunnels, was wrapped so thickly in bandages that Jake couldn't even tell if it was still swollen, or how well he could move his fingers if he tried. He had taken to looking away whenever Matt changed the bandages. The hand didn't hurt him at all. Molly had used her voice's power to stop the pain. That was all he cared about. And he had a feeling he really didn't want to know what his burned limb looked like now, if Matt's cursing and muttering about hospitals and specialists and stubborn, pig-headed idiots who refused to listen to basic medical advice, was any indication.

But worrying about how beat-up and shady he looked wouldn't make things any better. Jake pulled on a black hoodie and shoved his hands deep into the pockets.

"Ready," he announced, and plastered a fake smile on his face that he knew wouldn't fool Molly for a second. But she nodded and opened the door. Together, they stepped out into the hall.

BEA

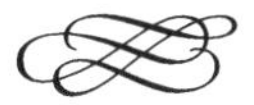

The angel held out his hand.

Practically naked, still bleeding a little from where broken pieces of her sailboat had struck against her head, Bea blinked and looked up at him.

The sun was shining behind him; his shoulder-length pale hair glowed golden. He wore no shirt, and the muscles of his arms and smooth chest were like perfect arches carved in pale white stone. He wore skin-tight pants of black leather and stood watching her expression warily, as though afraid she would turn down what was an obvious invitation to go with him. Where, Bea couldn't even begin to guess. His black wings stretched out behind him, strong and smooth, and as black as his black leather pants. She could see the veins and muscles that ran through his wings, round and thick as her arm. A single, small, sharp claw curled from their edges on either side. His brown eyes were both dark and kind. His chin was covered with blond stubble.

Bea knew she wasn't dreaming. He was too strange and glorious for her mind to have come up with this all on its own. Besides, it had been a long, long time since she had a dream this good.

No, this was really happening. She could feel the ground solid and real beneath her: grass and sand and sun-warmed stones. The sun shining off the waves in the distance was so bright that it hurt her eyes. She looked down at herself; the port from her chemo was still there. Her chest was a flattened valley of still-healing wounds and bunched uneven flesh.

"I'm not dead," Bea said again. This time the words weren't a question.

The angel nodded, and slowly lowered his hand. Bea looked away from him and out at the sea. She narrowed her eyes, trying to see into the distance, but she still couldn't see her sailboat anywhere. She wondered if it had been completely destroyed by the storm that had seemed so determined to drown her, or if the little ship had somehow escaped. She thought of the smooth wood of the deck, the crisp snap of the sails. Her throat constricted. Bea closed her eyes, shaking her head and refusing to let unruly emotion rise out of control. She would choose to believe that her boat was still out there: battered and partly broken, but still, somehow, bobbing up and down on the waves. Beautiful. Nearly whole. Free in a way she never would be.

She rubbed her eyes, ran her hands over her sore neck and her scratched, bare chest and arms.

"So what happened. Did you pull me out of the water?" Bea asked him.

The angel winced at the accusation in her voice. Eyes wide and uncertain, he nodded.

Suddenly Bea felt very, very tired. Grief and nausea welled in her chest.

"Well, you didn't do me any favors, then. Now I'll just have to find another way to end this." His smile disappeared, and he looked at her uncertainly. She motioned to her flat, scarred chest.

"I'm sick. See? I'm . . . I'm dying. The cancer is terminal. They've done everything that could be done, but none of it worked. You should have left me. It would have been easier that way. You should've just let me go."

Her words rang with anger, but she wasn't angry at him. She was angry at the cancer. At life. A life that seemed determined to torture her, to hold her down and force her to suffer in a million different, finely nuanced ways.

The angel crouched in front of her. Slowly, but with no hesitation, as though it were the most natural thing in the world, he reached out and touched her. He pressed his fingers, soft and cool, against her cheek and let them trail down her neck. Naturally, as though he had already touched her a thousand times, he let his fingers slide down to her chest. His touch was barely a whisper, his skin cool and soothing where it touched her ravaged skin. His fingers skimmed first across one scar, then the other.

A caress.

Bea had never expected to be caressed there, in the place where the cancer had attacked her, where the scars of a battle fought and lost stood out so starkly against the white of her skin.

His fingers were so gentle. Soothing.

Without thinking, she reached down and grabbed his hand, enclosing it in her own. She pulled his fingers to her lips and kissed them. His fingers tasted salty. Like the sea. He smelled like rain and sunshine. His hand was so large, and she leaned her head into his palm and closed her eyes.

"Thank you, anyway," she whispered after a moment, straightening up and clearing her throat to hide the emotion in her voice. "I know you meant well. Thank you for trying to help me. It isn't really your fault—it just turns out that nobody can."

They were silent for a long time. The angel hung his head, his eyes obscured by the sun-lit hair that fell over his face like a curtain. He almost looked like he was praying. Then, slowly, still holding her hand tightly in his own, the angel rose, pulling her to her feet after him.

Bea was so surprised that she didn't even try to pull away. She rose, standing barefoot in the sand.

The angel stepped forward, pressing the bare skin of his chest against hers.

Bea gasped. The warmth of his skin felt so good. She hadn't even realized she was cold. He wrapped his arms around her waist so tightly he lifted her off the ground.

Suddenly, Bea understood. She closed her eyes for a second.

Screw it, she whispered to herself. *Who cares what happens next? A gorgeous, shirtless man who doesn't talk wants to fly away with me. Who the fuck would say no to that?*

She wrapped her arms around his neck, holding him, resting her chin on his shoulder and squeezing her eyes shut.

"Just don't fucking drop me," she warned him, and she felt his chest vibrate with gentle laughter.

A sudden wind rose around them. When she felt the ground disappear from underneath her feet, she lifted her legs and clamped them tight around his waist. She could feel his wings moving, ever so slightly, up and down, up and down.

It reminded her of sailing.

JAKE

Things had changed a lot since Steele's invasion of the Refuge. Molly had told the Echoes that they had to make their underground home into a fortress, and they really took her words to heart. Echoes patrolled the halls in pairs of two, their eyes probing every corner, inspecting the face of every person who walked past. The gas lanterns that were spaced out every few feet along the tunnel had been turned up as high as they would go so that they exposed bronze pipes covering the ceiling. The lanterns flooded every inch of the passageway with a rosy red light so bright that it forced all the shadows away, and left the intricately tiled floors tinged with red.

The biggest difference, though, was in the faces of the people they passed as they walked toward Andrew's rooms. Before, Jake remembered the feeling of discomfort that would creep down his neck as he walked among the Echoes. He was among them, but not one of them, and every time he met someone's eyes, it was clear that everyone around him was always conscious of that fact. That feeling had disappeared. Jake wasn't sure if it was because word had spread about what Steele had done to him, and his experience had, in their eyes, earned him an honorary place among them. Or, it might just be, with the new threat that seemed to loom above them all the time, the Echoes had no more time to worry or care that Jake had taken up residence in the Refuge.

They reached the arched iron door of Andrew's room. It had been left propped open, and Molly leaned inside.

"Have you got a minute, Andrew?" she called out. "I've got an update for you."

"Of course! Come right on in!" Andrew answered, the warm silk of his voice making Jake shudder. He walked toward them as they entered, his hands held out in greeting. Andrew had always had a slightly unkempt look. His chin-length red hair tended to fall into his face, and he always seemed to have a shadow of red stubble edging his face. But since Steele's attack, dark bags had gathered under Andrew's eyes. The stubble on his chin had lengthened and grown thicker. His blue eyes, which had always sparkled with excitement and a bit of smugness before, had grown a bit hazy from lack of sleep. And Andrew's study was a disaster. Half-empty coffee cups lined every inch of available table space, of which there was very little. Open books, scattered papers, and high stacks of printed paper filled every corner of his space. The walls were covered with maps, drawings, and notecards lined with his tight, furious scrawl.

"Are you doing okay, Andrew?" Molly asked, her eyes widening a little as she looked slowly around the room. "Maybe you need to get some sleep."

Andrew's warm smile faltered. "I'm fine," he answered, a little too sharply. He seemed to bite back a longer reply, looking down as he rubbed his forehead. "There's just too much to do. We can't afford to waste time." He pulled out a map and tapped it anxiously with his finger. "The entrance to the cave is covered by water. Apparently, there is only one day a month that the water recedes far enough for the opening to be accessible. The day after the full moon: that's two weeks from now. We can't afford to waste time; I've got to try for it then. Steele is hot on the heels of this thing. If he finds another way in, or figures out a way to get to it before I do . . ." He looked up at Molly expectantly. "What did you find out from Lena? Tell me everything."

Jake hung back, watching Andrew's face carefully as Molly described what had happened. Andrew's eyes hardened, his lips pressed tight. His hands balled into fists at his sides.

"So you didn't learn a single thing that can help us," Andrew cut in, as Molly's story was drawing to a close.

Molly's shoulders stiffened, but when she answered there was no heat in her voice.

"Not really," she admitted. "I think Lena is just too determined to have nothing to do with us."

"And so the three of you just let her walk off?" Andrew folded his arms over his chest, his eyes boring into Molly's. "You didn't do anything more?"

Jake edged closer to Molly, till he was standing right at her elbow. He didn't like the way that, when Andrew's charming expressions and friendly smiles disintegrated, they left something cold and hungry in their place.

"What more were we supposed to do?" Molly demanded. "We tried as hard as we could to convince her."

"There were three of you, and two of them," Andrew pointed out, his eyebrows climbing. "And your voice is one of the most powerful we have."

Aww shit, Jake thought to himself. *Now things are going to get ugly.*

"You wanted me to try to *force* her?" Molly cried. Her face flushed. "You can't be serious, Andrew. Who the hell do you think I am? I wouldn't call Lena fragile, exactly, but it is pretty freaking clear that she's been through a lot. There's no way I would even *think* about using my voice to make her do something she didn't want to."

"Lena is one person," Andrew replied. "I am trying to keep our entire group alive. She might have information that would make that possible. And you just let her walk away."

Molly shook her head in disbelief, raising her hands and leaning away from Andrew, as though she needed as much air between them as possible. "I seriously can't believe what I'm hearing right now. No wonder Lena fucking hates you if that's the way you think about things."

"I'm doing what I need to do to keep us alive."

Molly's eyebrows bunched together. She leaned in closer to Andrew and lowered her voice.

"You are being an asshole, Andrew. *That's* what you're doing. I gave you Evie's USB key to help you find this goblet of yours. But sometimes you make me wonder if I should have just smashed it instead."

Andrew's face flushed, and his nostrils flared. "I think this conversation is over," he said, his voice cold with suppressed fury.

"Oh, don't worry. I've got nothing more to say to you," Molly hissed, spinning on her heel and grabbing Jake's hand as she stormed out the door.

The iron door clanged shut behind them.

"I cannot believe that bullshit!" Molly fumed. A few Echoes who were hurrying by, most likely on their way to dinner, turned their heads in her direction, their eyes lighting up with curiosity. Molly bit her lip and turned so that she stood facing away from them. "Did he honestly think I would use my voice on Lena like that?" she asked Jake in an outraged whisper.

"If he did, then he doesn't know you very well." Jake ran a hand up and down Molly's arm. Just having the shut door between them and Andrew let him breathe a little easier. "Let's go and get some food. I bet that'll make you feel better."

"I can't go to the Tavern right now," Molly grimaced and shoved her hands deep into the pockets of her jeans. "If I do, I'll just complain to Matt and Thia, and they both think Andrew walks on water." Her lips curved upward into a mischievous smile.

"Let's go out," she said with a conspiratorial grin. "Like, really out. Janice and the band are playing the Homeland bar tonight. Let's go see the show."

"I thought Andrew wanted everybody to lay low," Jake answered slowly. "I thought unnecessary trips out of the Refuge had to wait until Steele isn't a threat anymore."

"And who knows how long that will be?" Molly asked, shaking her head. "We need a break; even if it's just for a few hours. This place is going to make me lose my mind, and you've been cooped up in our room for so long while your back healed. You need to get out and get some fresh air, and so do I. It'll do us both good."

"Molly . . ." Jake swallowed. Just the thought of going back out into the world made his palms sweaty with a mixture of panic and desire. Down here, the Refuge wrapped around him like a cocoon, a constant torment and protection. His craving never subsided, but he at least knew that he couldn't actually *get* the drugs. On the surface . . . anything could happen. "I just don't think you should piss Andrew off any more than you already have. He seems pretty on edge, and he isn't the kind of guy you want angry with you."

"But how will he even know?" Molly asked in a stage whisper. She took Jake's hand in both of hers and backed down the hallway, towing him behind her. Jake dragged his feet. "Come on. It'll be fun," she coaxed him. "I managed to get a message to Janice last week. I told her that my cousin died and that I had to go out of town all of a sudden. But now I'm back and, even though I'm still kind of broken up and not feeling up to singing, I might stop by anyway."

"It just . . ." Jake pulled them both to a stop, "seems like a risky thing to do."

"You've been down here for weeks, Jake," Molly said, and Jake could see the worry starting to surface in her eyes. "Don't you *want* to go out?" Molly stepped closer to him. "What's the matter?"

He should just tell her, Jake thought. Tell her that his addiction was a parasite, still tunneled deep inside him, tearing at his insides. Poisoning his blood.

He looked at her.

Her eyes were so beautiful. Dread swirled like a cyclone in his heart. At any moment those eyes would harden. The warm hand that felt so right in his would pull away. And Jake knew, right down to his core, that the cold of being all alone again would kill him.

"Nothing's wrong!" Jake cried, tightening his fingers around hers. He stepped closer to her, and brushed her long hair over her shoulder, trailing his fingers along her neck. "It sounds great. Let's go."

Molly looked at him, her eyes searching his face. Jake forced his smile to widen. After a second, Molly seemed satisfied. She turned, and they started walking together toward the elevator.

Jake let out a long, quiet breath that hissed between his teeth. Molly knew him better than anyone. If she really wanted to break down his walls and see through his fakes smiles, she could. But Jake knew how easy it was to swallow a lie you wanted to believe.

"And don't worry. I won't sing. The last time I performed, and my voice got out of control, I almost caused a freaking stampede. I'm not stupid enough to do that again." Molly glanced over at him, her eyes sparkling with laughter. "It'll be hard to listen to Janice singing all my songs. But you'll be there. If I lose it and start to go up on stage and make a grab for the microphone, you'll just have to tackle me to the ground and drag me off before it's too late." She laughed at her own joke.

Jake stopped short. It took Molly half a step before she realized he wasn't next to her. "What's the matter, Jake?" She asked, her eyebrows climbing.

"It's just that . . . you might not want to say stuff like that to me."

"What? Why not?" She came and lay a hand against his chest. "I'm just joking around."

"Yeah, but . . . if you tell me to do something, I'm gonna to do it. I won't have a choice." Jake watched as his words sank in. The easy laughter in Molly's eyes evaporated. Something that looked an awful lot like fear took its place.

"Sometimes," Jake said quietly, "you forget what you can do to me."

Molly swallowed. "I think I forget it almost all of the time." She looked down at her shoes, as though her ability was something to be ashamed of. "Most of the time, I don't want to remember."

"Can you *please* not forget?" Jake ran a hand across his forehead. "I trust you, Molly. I really, really do. But sometimes, I feel like we're in a little over our heads with this stuff."

"I know," Molly whispered. She leaned in and wrapped her arms around his neck. He pulled her against him, and for a moment they clung to each other, tight; as though the world was a storm trying to rip them apart.

"I'll be more careful," Molly whispered in his ear. "I promise."

And then the moment was over. They stepped apart without meeting each other's eyes. Jake forced a smile, and they walked briskly toward the exit.

Riding the metro was torturous.

Jake hated the noise, the push of unfamiliar people all around him. Twice, bile rose in his throat and he fought it down, feeling sweat bead on his forehead. There was too much life here, too much bustle. Jake felt like the sides of the metro were metal coffin walls, pressing in on him. The darkness of the tunnels and the lights that shot by them through the windows were eerie and alien. The babble of voices around him made his head swim.

"Two more stops," Molly commented, leaning in close so that he could hear her over the noise. Jake had to resist the urge to wrap his arm around her middle, cling to her, and beg her to take him back to the little room they shared. He wasn't ready to be out here. He wasn't fit to be in the real world. This had been a terrible mistake.

"Sounds good," he answered, and turned to look out the window so she couldn't see his face. His reflection stared back at him; pale skin and dark eyes. Another version of himself—a phantom Jake who was whole, and worthy of affection.

When they stepped off the train, Molly casually slipped her hand through his, leading him through the crowd, breaking a path for him through the masses of people. Leading him down the street, and into the crowded bar.

They found seats in the back just as the music started. Jake could see how much it hurt Molly not to be on stage. Janice sang well, but it was nothing like what Molly could have done, nowhere near the way she could have set that room on fire. Her lips were a thin line as she watched. Sometimes she looked away, as though the sight of what she loved but could no longer have was too much for her to take.

Jake knew exactly how she felt.

When the show was over, it was Tim who spotted her through the crowd.

"Our captain has returned!" he hollered, pushing his way through the crowd with some difficulty and wrapping a thick arm around her neck. "What are you doing hiding out back here? Come! Come with me! Mike and Janice are backstage and we all want to see you!"

"I can't Tim, not tonight . . ."

But Tim wasn't listening, just pulling her along as he turned and headed toward the back.

"Will you be alright?" Molly called, looking back at Jake.

Jake wanted to shout out to her not to leave him alone. He wanted to wrap his arms around her waist, press his face into her stomach, and beg her not to leave him all alone. But then she would know.

"I'll be fine!" he shouted, not even sure that she could hear him through the crowd.

"I'll be back in a bit!" she yelled back, and then she was gone.

He put his elbows on the bar, determined not to turn around and look behind him, but that lasted for only a minute or two.

He was alone now. Nothing stood between him and what he wanted.

That awareness brought the hunger roaring to the surface of his brain. And so it was with dread, but also with a certain amount of resignation, that Jake turned around and let his eyes run over the room.

It wasn't hard to find. Like a bloodhound, he was attuned to certain cues that most people couldn't see. He knew how to sniff out what others couldn't.

He shuddered and sighed. This was always how it was going to be. He wasn't surprised, or even disappointed, really. It was just reality coming back after a brief hiatus. A beautiful, sweet dream, despite the fear and pain that shot through it. A delirious hallucination in which someone beautiful and whole reached out for him, protected him. Believed in him. It had been a wonderful dream . . . but in the end, it was nothing more than that. It didn't even take a minute for him to know where the drugs were, didn't take more than another minute to cross the room to the dark corner where he knew they could be found. It was like a neon sign with a giant flashing arrow, calling him to the place that he needed to go. He knew a couple of the other junkies; they nodded to him as he joined the little, clustered group. The rest were strangers to him, but they all were family in a sense. They all had the same tightness in their jaw, the same need shining in their eye. And they would all turn on each other in an instant; steal, rob, beat each other black and blue if it meant getting more of what they needed. Just like a real family.

Jake smiled and pulled up a chair. This was comfortable. He was home.

EVIE

"*I can't believe I agreed to bring you here,*" Roman signed, his face bleak, his forehead damp with sweat. His black wings drooped behind him, as though in anticipation of defeat.

Evie looked away from him. She could feel hairs rising along the back of her neck. Every time she looked over at him, a fresh wave of shock rolled through her.

She had thought that she knew him. She had thought that her feelings for him were based on something real. But he had been lying to her from the first moment they met. She edged away, putting a little more space between them. If Roman noticed, at least he didn't say anything.

She swallowed hard, looking around her. To say that her life had spun suddenly and completely out of control was a laughable understatement. She folded her hands under her arms so that Roman wouldn't see the way they shook.

"Where are we?" she asked. It felt so strange to speak out loud to Roman, instead of signing. But his deafness had been an act—just another layer of lies that he had told her. A way for him to avoid using his voice and enthralling any nearby human. She refused to sign to him, now that she knew the truth.

"I can't tell you that!" Roman's hands jumped with agitation as he responded. *"The rest of the Sirens are going to want to kill you on sight anyway, simply for invading our home! Knowing its location would only make things worse!"*

Suspicion surged inside her, and Evie forced it down with difficulty. As much as she knew that Roman had brought her here because she insisted on it, it was hard not to fear him. For as long as she could remember, growing up in a Legacy household, she had heard stories of the Watchers. They were the bogeymen who had haunted her dreams; the great, dangerous beasts that all Legacy children knew to fear. People said they feasted on human flesh. They spoke in whispers of the fate, worse than death, that lay in store for any Legacy that was caught disobeying their rules. Even later, when Evie began her feverish research and started to hope that at least some of the stories she had grown up with were not exactly true . . . still. She had imagined their home to be a place of crumbling stone and dark shadow, fetid air and echoing cobweb-filled halls.

But this was beautiful.

The ocean stretched out behind them, an endless expanse of turquoise and green, the sun dancing on its surface like a million crystals scattered by a generous hand. The edges of the cave actually stood several feet deep in the water. But it wasn't like any cave Evie had seen, in life or in pictures. The cave was filled with light—the ceiling of it opened up in a large circle, and even the sides were in large, curved doorways that made her think of a circus tent, made of golden stone. Sunlight poured in and pressed itself against every crevice. Looking up through the opening at the pale blue sky beyond, Evie knew that, at night, the spacious cave would be filled with moonlight. The damp sand under her feet was smooth and perfect, as though no human foot had tread on it in a thousand years. A tingle of fear inched up her spine as she realized that might actually be the case.

"This entrance is not used often," Roman explained, seeing her

expression. *"It is for free-humans to use. No one like that has entered our home in living memory."* He shook his head, his eyes full of dread. *"Until today."*

Evie nodded and swallowed hard, hoping that the fear swirling in her belly wasn't evident on her face.

"You know we will both probably die today, right?" Roman asked, stepping closer to her so that when he signed his fingers brushed up against her arm. *"You for your trespass, and me, for showing you the way in?"*

Evie swallowed hard and wrapped her arms around her middle. "They'll listen to us," she insisted, trying to believe it. "They have to."

Roman nodded slowly, then turned and walked toward the back of the cave. Evie followed behind him, watching the way that the tips of his wings left twin tracks in the sand.

The opening was barely big enough for Roman to fit through, and even without wings, Evie felt her breath hitch as she lowered herself in. She had never thought of herself as claustrophobic, but her throat still tightened with fear as she wiggled, with sand at her back and the stone wall only inches from her face, through a dim, unknown tunnel.

When her feet finally came out into open air, she felt Roman's hands reaching up to help her find her footing as she slid free.

As soon as her feet touched solid ground, she bounded away from his touch. His fingers pulled back instantly, as though he felt ashamed for daring to touch her.

"What is this place?" Evie whispered.

Roman's lips quirked upward in an ironic smile. *"The visitor's entrance,"* he signed.

They had emerged into a hollowed-out mountain, or a volcano that had long been dormant. Now a secret garden flourished in the hollowed-out depths. Trees grew thickly from the stone wall, their trunks curving gracefully upward, toward the sun. The deep green of their foliage splashed, lush against the slate gray stone.

Birdsong echoed faintly from somewhere up above. High above them, the gray circling stone opened into a wide circle that dripped thick, hanging moss. The blue sky peered down at them through the opening, seemingly a hundred miles away.

A broad, stone-paved path wove up a small hill and led to an open-air pavilion built of bamboo, wood, and stone. She and Roman walked up the path and, with each step, Evie felt herself leaving forever the life that she had known. Painted bright red and gold, the pavilion had no doors, and other than sunlight and brisk, chilling wind, it contained only one thing.

The gong that hung in the center of the pavilion was as big as Evie was tall. Perfect, unvarnished silver, it was inscribed all over with writing in a language Evie had never seen. A long mallet hung beside it, swinging slightly in the breeze.

Roman and Evie stood together, in front of the gong. Neither of them moved.

The shine of its silver was so perfect that Evie could see her own reflection, grim and unsmiling, staring back at her. Five-foot-nothing, her wind-tossed black curls fell, unruly, into her eyes. The freckles, sprinkled liberally across the light-brown skin of her face, spread across the bridge of her nose and her cheeks, making her look young—too young. Almost like a child.

Evie hadn't felt like a child in a long, long time.

She bit her lip, suddenly uncertain. She certainly didn't look like someone who could coolly force herself into a hidden, supernatural world, full of powers she couldn't equal and rules she didn't understand. Evie looked back, over her shoulder.

The path was open behind her.

"We can still turn back," Roman signed to her, seeming to read her mind.

Evie shook her head. She took a deep breath and pushed her hair behind her ears. She reached up and lifted the mallet from its hook. It was heavier than she expected. She wrapped her fingers around it, feeling its weight on her palms.

She stared back at the gong with narrowed eyes, as though daring her reflection to try to dissuade her from her chosen course. Her own eyes stared back at her, their deep brown color glinting with determination, and brimming with the kind of knowledge that only life's harshest lessons can bestow.

Troy had wanted to break her. Evie stared at her reflection. She hadn't let him break her then. And she wouldn't let the memory of him stop her now.

Evie knew perfectly well that if she rang this gong, she could never go back; not to the world that she had known, or the life that had been hers. Everything would change. Roman seemed pretty sure they would die.

But life had already taught her that there are far worse things than dying.

She had been through some of them already. At a certain point, she thought, you get so used to fear that you stop letting it control you. You simply do what needs to be done.

Evie hefted the mallet high in the air and struck the gong, over and over again, with all her strength.

MOLLY

Molly smiled at the guys as they walked down the hall together but, inside, she felt like screaming.

The Homeland bar was just the way she remembered it: scratched-up tables, a rowdy, jostling crowd. The air filled with smoke, laughter, and the icy wind that streamed through the propped open door. She could feel the music thrumming inside her, like a caged animal pacing; desperate to get out.

How had she lost this?

This place had been better than a home—it had been where she belonged. She missed the warm press of the stage lights against her skin like a physical loss. She had found a kind of freedom and an expansive, wild peace, every time she stepped on to that stage.

Now she couldn't imagine ever standing on that stage again.

Mike and Tim were arguing as they headed down the hallway to a shabby back room that all the band members shared.

"Tim, seriously man, you're delusional. That blonde was looking right at me. She couldn't look away. I'm sorry to crush your dreams, but . . ." Mike patted him on the back. "You've got to face reality, brother. I'm hotter than you. Deal with it."

Janice looked over her shoulder just long enough to roll her eyes at both of them. Slender, and so short that the top of her head barely reached Tim's shoulder, she still managed to make it clear that *they* were the childish ones.

"Bullshit." Tim snorted dismissively. "Women always want the drummer. It's practically a scientific fact. It's the rhythm . . . it turns them on. They know that if we can make rhythm like that on stage . . ." Tim gyrated his substantial hips suggestively, and Mike roared with laughter.

"I'm not kidding you!" Tim insisted. "There's a reason my bed is so big. And it isn't just this." He patted his prominent stomach contentedly.

"Could you guys, please, just shut up?" Janice hissed. Shoulders hunched forward, she kicked open the door of the dressing room and slumped down heavily into one of the chairs. "You're giving me a freaking headache."

Molly glanced at her sharply. Janice usually got right into the middle of all the boys' arguments. But Janice's tightly curled black hair fell down around the edges of her face, hiding her eyes.

"So, where you been, Molly?" Tim asked, sitting down and propping his feet up on an empty chair. "You just ran off and left us! Janice said you had a cousin that died and had to go out of town all of a sudden?"

"Yeah, it was real sad," Molly answered. "But you guys are doing fine without me! Janice was awesome tonight!"

She looked to Janice, expecting to see a sparkle in her eyes and one of her broad grins. Instead, Janice kept her eyes down, her arms crossed tightly over her stomach. Molly's smile faded. She looked at Janice more closely. She hadn't noticed before, but now . . .

"Guys!" Molly interrupted Mike and Tim's new argument. "You must be hungry, after the show. You should go get something to eat."

"Damn, Molly!" Mike whined, sitting down and staring at her

resentfully. "Why you got to mother-hen us all the time? I just want to sit down and chat with you . . . that's all."

"I'll buy," Molly offered bluntly, pulling a twenty from her pocket and holding it up in the air. Mike jumped right back out of the chair.

"But you're a fucking *awesome* mother hen!" he exclaimed, snatching the bill from her fingers and throwing his arm around Tim's shoulders. "Come, my friend," he said. "I feel a deep and primal need for chicken wings. Can we bring you ladies anything?" He was all chivalry, now that he wasn't paying.

"No," Molly answered when Janice didn't so much as look up. "Just get out. Now."

She followed behind them, practically shoving them out the door, and closed the door tightly behind them. She turned.

"Janice?"

Janice didn't answer or look up. Dread built in Molly's chest. She walked over and crouched down in front of Janice's chair.

"It's okay," Molly said softly. "You know you can tell me."

Janice looked up, and now Molly could see the faint purple of bruises just beneath the thick stage make-up that Janice didn't usually wear.

"He came back," Janice whispered hoarsely, tears gathering in her eyes. "I fucking hate myself. I'm such an idiot, Molly."

"Kevin's back?" Molly gasped, and Janice nodded. "Oh my God. How bad are you hurt?"

"Pretty bad!" Janice exclaimed and burst into tears. Molly wrapped her arms around her tentatively, afraid to hug her too tight.

"I swore to myself," Janice moaned, her face pressed against Molly's shoulder. "I absolutely swore to myself that I'd never let this be my life again. That I'd call 911 if I so much as saw his face. That I'd be smarter. But he knows all the right things to say. And I *do* blame myself for some of it, no matter what anybody says. And he seemed so sincere this time, so sweet. He promised it'd be different, that we could make it work." For a minute Janice's words were lost in deep, wrenching sobs. She wiped her eyes with the back of her hand. "I'm just so, so stupid."

"You are *not* stupid," Molly said fiercely. "You are smart, and talented and amazing in a hundred different ways. Janice, really."

Janice peered out from behind her fingers.

Molly took a deep breath. No amount of time would ever make some things easy to remember or to say. "You know I've been there," she said softly.

Janice bit her lip and nodded.

"It isn't about smart, or strong, or anything like that," Molly continued. "You are all of those things." Molly took a deep breath. "Did you kick him out?"

Janice hid her face in her hands. "You don't understand," she said, her voice shaking, "it's even worse than it was before. I've never been this scared. He took my house keys. My credit cards. For the last two weeks, he's been following me wherever I go. And . . . it isn't just that he gets mad. He's smart about it now. Look. He tries to hit me in places where no one will see." She pulled up the corner of her shirt, and Molly bit back a gasp.

Janice's side was a mass of black and purple bruises. Janice winced as she twisted to look down at her injuries, and pressed a tentative hand against her side. "I think he broke a rib," she whispered. "Maybe two."

Molly felt the room swim around her. She looked away quickly, closing her eyes. Trying to breathe. She felt the blood rushing to her face, and her ears rung. Fury rose in her throat.

It burned.

She loved Janice. And suddenly she hated this man who had hurt her with an equal fierceness.

"You have to kick him out," Molly said, fighting to keep her voice calm.

"I can't! I'm not kidding, Molly. He'll kill me."

"You can. Mike and Tim and I will help," Molly said, rubbing

Janice's knee. "We'll make sure you're safe—we won't let him touch you. I'll give you the keys to my place. You can stay there as long as you want. We'll make sure you have everything you need." But Janice was shaking her head vehemently.

"I can't," she whispered. "I'm afraid. Really, truly afraid, Molly."

Molly didn't think about it as she put her hands on Janice's shoulders and clamped down. It happened, as naturally and simply as drawing breath.

"Don't be," she said, her voice thick with layers of power. "You can do this. *Don't be afraid."*

Janice stared at her. "But I am."

Molly blinked. It should be working.

"Don't be," she said again, her eyes pushing into Janice's, her voice rasping with the force of her effort.

Janice pulled back, looking at her strangely. "What's the matter with you, Molly?" she asked uncertainly. "Why is your voice all funny like that?"

Molly rocked back on her heels, shock and frustration flooding her. Her voice had failed her. What had she done wrong?

Mike and Tim were back. Their voices loud and boisterous in the hall, their footsteps close.

"Is Kevin here?" Molly asked quickly, in an undertone.

"Yes," Janice answered automatically. "He didn't want Mike or Tim to know he's back in town, so he's waiting for me out back. But I don't . . ."

"We have returned!" Mike announced, setting several beers down on the table with a bang. "And we come bearing libations."

Molly sprang to her feet, pushing past them and out the door. It slammed shut behind her. She heard them calling out to her, but didn't turn back. She knew this bar well enough to weave her way to the back entrance with little trouble. She darted around the people, not really seeing anyone.

In her mind, she could only see her own demons.

She threw herself through the back door and stumbled out in

the dirty back alley. The cold night air greeted her, and the full of the rich aromas of the overflowing trashcans that lined the dark back side of the street. The harvest moon hung pale yellow above her and seemed to stare down at Molly, following her every move.

Kevin stood in the shadows, his face lit with the red glow of the half-finished cigarette that dangled from his lips. It had been almost a year since Molly had last seen him, but she hadn't forgotten the sharp lines of his face or the cool, calculating look of his eyes. He wore a gleaming leather jacket, that had to be brand new, over his broad shoulders and meaty arms. Molly wondered if he'd bought it with one of Janice's credit cards. The dark eyes that had drawn Janice in, and managed to fool her for a while, snapped over to Molly's face.

Taking in her expression, he sneered at her.

"What's got your panties in a knot, bitch?" he asked. "Has Janice been blubbering to you?" He dropped his cigarette and crushed it with the heel of his shoe. Throwing his shoulders back, he stepped closer to her. Built like a football player, he towered over her, at least a hundred pounds heavier than her, most of it in muscle.

Molly took a deep, steadying breath of the frigid night air, and smiled.

Her fingers tightened on the handle of a nearby metal trashcan lid.

"What the fuck do you want?" Kevin demanded.

Molly stepped forward, bringing the lid up in a graceful arc, slamming it full force into his face.

"I want you to scream," she said sweetly as he stumbled backward, blood streaming from his nose.

MOLLY

Kevin clutched at his bloody nose as he stumbled backward, yelling with surprise and fury.

He reached out and ripped the lid from her hands.

"You're going to fucking regret that," he said, spitting blood out onto the pavement. He moved toward her, pulling back his fist. Molly fell back a step. If her voice didn't work this time, he would probably kill her.

She held her hand out, palm first, in front of her, and reached deep inside, to the place where emotion and imagination lived.

She felt her power there. Waiting, like a gun ready to fire.

"Freeze!" she screamed at him.

Instantly, his joints froze. His limbs locked in place. He stood, statue-like, before her. She reached out and pulled the trashcan lid carefully from his fingers.

His eyes bulged. His breath came fast and hard. But he didn't move.

Then Molly picked up right where she had left off.

She moved in a haze of pain and fury, striking again and again. Hating him. Hating everyone like him. The anger in the pit of her stomach was so hot that it scorched her insides, and made her arm move as though of its own accord. She didn't stop until it occurred to her that she might easily kill him.

Her arm stilled. She stared at him.

He hadn't made much noise . . . his lips were still frozen. But his eyes had changed. There was no anger in them now, no threat. All she could see was absolute terror. Molly let the lid fall from numb fingers, clattering onto the pavement. It was hard for her to look at his face.

"Keys," she said, holding out a hand, and letting the power of her voice flow through her. *"Give me Janice's keys. And anything else you have that belongs to her."*

He moved stiffly, as though his joints were barely thawed. He pulled keys and credit cards from his pockets and dropped them into Molly's open palm.

"Good," Molly said. She licked her lips, then hoped that he hadn't noticed the nervous gesture. She had never tested her power in quite this way. It was mostly a bluff. But, she knew that, at his core, Kevin was a coward. And if she played this right, he would walk out of this alley fearing her the way the pious fear their God. *"Now. Listen to me. You will stay away from Janice. Forever. You will never touch her, talk to her, or see her again. Ever. Do you understand?"*

Kevin nodded frantically.

"Good. Remember what happened tonight. And if you ever hurt another woman again, I'll know it. And I will find you." It was a lie. And Molly was pretty sure that any control her voice might have over his actions would fade, given some time. But Kevin didn't know that. He nodded again. *"Remember, anytime I want, I can have you on your knees. And don't fucking test me. It'll be the last thing you ever do."*

Kevin whimpered, low in his throat.

"Now get the hell out of here."

Kevin turned and, limping, scrambled down the street.

Molly watched him run. Then she turned and walked back into the bar.

She found Tim, his arm around a tipsy, overly affectionate woman with long blond hair.

"Come," she said, grabbing his arm and pulling him away.

"Hey!" he protested. "We're in the middle of a very important conversation here!"

"It'll wait," Molly growled and glanced at the woman. "Sorry," she said, but the woman just gave a shrug and teetered away. "Listen," Molly told Tim, who at least wasn't drunk yet. "Kevin came back."

"You're kidding me." In an instant, all the levity disappeared from Tim's face.

"Yup. Two weeks ago."

"Two weeks?" Tim's eyebrows shot up. "Why didn't she tell us?"

"Because he beat her so bad that she was afraid he'd kill her."

"Shit." Tim's face flushed bright red.

"I scared him off," Molly told him, ignoring his look of surprise. "But I still don't think that Janice should be by herself. I'd stay if I could, but I've got a lot of other stuff going on right now." Mentally, Molly patted herself on the back for not adding, 'and a bunch of people want to kill me right now, so it's probably better for everyone if I keep my distance.' Molly pulled Janice's keys out of her pocket. "This is her stuff that Kevin had. Her keys and credit cards. And here's the key to my apt." Molly set everything down on the bar. "Why don't you take her to my place and let her rest up for a bit. Kind of keep an eye on her."

Tim picked up Janice's stuff but handed Molly's keys back to her.

"No offense Molly," he said, "but your apartment is kind of a dump. She can crash at my place for as long as she needs."

"You're sure?" Molly asked. She knew that would be better for a bunch of reasons, but hadn't wanted to ask too much of Tim.

"Course."

"You're amazing."

"Obviously," Tim agreed. He craned his head to the side, "I'm gonna go find her and get her out of here. The crowd tonight is pretty lame anyway."

"Okay," Molly said, then hesitated."And, Tim. You won't . . . hit on her, right? She's been through a lot."

Tim's eyebrows shot up. "Of course not!" he cried, indignantly. "Janice is like my kid sister. I hit on her *friends,* Molly. Not on her."

He grinned at Molly's slightly dumbfounded expression and, with a wink, turned and walked away.

With one worry at least momentarily taken care of, Molly began to search the crowd for Jake. She hadn't meant to leave him alone for so long, and she couldn't ignore the feeling of worry that kept flaring in her chest.

She couldn't see him anywhere. But she knew he hadn't left.

The third time her eyes raked the room, she saw the darkened hallway, marked only by a burned-out bulb, swaying in an invisible breeze.

Suddenly, she knew.

In an instant, she had crossed the crowded room and rushed down the dirty, black passageway.

There, slouched against locked doors, she found a small circle of haggard people with vacant eyes. Jake was with them. There was a needle in his hand.

"Jake!" Molly would have been horrified if she could have believed what she was seeing. But it didn't quite seem real. Jake had been doing so well! He had seemed completely better! "What the hell are you doing?"

They looked at each other, and Molly felt despair twist inside her. But there was no fresh mark on Jake's scarred arm. She wasn't too late.

"*Come on,* Jake," she said firmly, trying to keep her voice from shaking. "*We're leaving.*"

He stood immediately, as she knew he would. She stormed out with him right beside her. As soon as they reached the street, she turned to face him, a hundred different accusations on her lips.

Then she realized the needle was still in his hand.

"What is wrong with you, Jake?" she cried, her voice edging toward a scream. "Drop that thing!"

He stared back at her, his eyes swimming with emotions she couldn't understand. Sweat broke out on his forehead, and his fingers twitched.

But he didn't drop the needle.

"Molly . . ." he grunted, his voice rasping, "you have to leave me."

"What?" Molly squinted at him. Had she been wrong? Was he high already? What he was saying didn't make sense. "I don't understand."

"I know you don't," he laughed, the sound hollow and bitter. "That's the problem. Did you really think it would be that easy? That you could make everything better just like that? A few days getting sober, a good long sleep . . . and then, all of a sudden, everything would be alright?"

He took a step closer to her. She could see tears glinting in the corners of his eyes. He still clutched the needle in one hand. With his other hand, he reached up to touch her face. "You don't know. Someone like you—you couldn't possibly imagine what it's like to be as damaged as I am. I'm in love with you, Molly. Between that, and that voice of yours, you've got a big hold over me. You could make me do a lot of stuff if you wanted to. Almost anything."

She started to speak, but he shook his head sharply, and the words died in her throat.

"But even with all that power and all that love . . ." he looked away from her, and the words choked out, "I'm a mess deep inside, in places that your power doesn't go. You can make my body do anything that you want but my mind, Molly, and my soul—they're the most messed up of all. Deep down, it's like all I'm made up of is broken glass. If you saw that, for real . . . if you knew how messed up I really am, or some of the things I've done . . . you wouldn't want me. And you'd be right."

He shook his head. "It's been so good, these weeks with you. So very, very good. But all that's over now. Now you have to know the truth."

"But . . . Couldn't I . . ."

"Couldn't you what?" Jake's voice snapped with sudden anger. "Are you going to order me to stay in our bedroom in the Refuge forever, Molly? Maybe tell me to sit on my hands? Tie a leash around my neck if we ever have to go out in public, just so you'll be sure that I'll stay clean? Do you want your voice to be a cage that holds me for the rest of my life?"

"Of course not!" Molly gasped. "I want to help you, Jake. To cure you. Not to make you a prisoner."

"That's what you have to understand," he said, his voice grating. He leaned in toward her, his eyes wide and glistening. "There is no cure. Not for me. There never will be." He looked down at the needle in his hand. "It's time for you to walk away."

"And what happens then, Jake?" Molly swallowed hard against the sob building in her throat. "If I walk away right now, and leave you here? Tell me."

"I die." He answered simply, his face showing no emotion at all. "That's the only way this is going to end. I've known that for a long time. It might happen tonight. Maybe in a week. It won't be long. Not now, when I've been missing it so much . . ."

He could have punched her in the stomach and it would have hurt less. Hearing Jake talk about his own death so calmly was the worst thing that Molly had ever heard.

"No." Molly reached down and pried the syringe from Jake's fingers. She hurled it down on the cement and stomped on it with the heel of her boot. "That isn't going to happen. I won't let it. It isn't too late, Jake. Not for you, and not for us. I'm not giving up on you. Come with me now. We're going home."

BEA

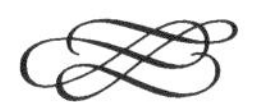

The last thing Bea would have expected to do while being flown through the air in the arms of a winged man who looked like a Calvin Klein model was sleep. But she did. She had not slept for days while on the ship, and the concussion to her head made everything wavy around the edges. The angel's arms were smooth and tight around her, her legs curled around his waist securely.

"Maybe I'll die now," she thought to herself as she drifted off, "and wake when he's carried me to heaven."

The thought made her smile and, smiling, she slept.

She woke on a sandy shore with the ocean stretching broad and deep before her. The sun was blistering hot on her sensitive skin. The angel held her shoulders to keep her steady on her feet as she blinked and gazed around to get her bearings. She felt a little lightheaded, and not entirely sure that she wasn't dreaming.

They were in front of a lighthouse. It towered up above them: white with broad red stripes. Three stone steps led up to the lighthouse's red painted door, which was rounded at the top. The angel watched her closely, holding onto her arms, making sure she wouldn't fall when he let go of her. Bea smiled up at him.

"No, really," she said, wishing her voice sounded steadier. "I'm fine."

He raised one eyebrow in disbelief, and then let go, still holding his hands out as though ready to catch her if she crumpled. When he saw that she was alright, he held up one finger in front of him. Bea didn't understand.

"What?" she started to ask, but he held up the finger again, then leaped up the stairs, opened the door and walked into the lighthouse, closing the door firmly behind him.

Bea stared after him, totally confused.

She heard some sounds from behind the door—a sound like hands clapping, and then feet scuffling on stone. She would have wondered more fiercely what was going on if she hadn't been so tired. As it was, she just looked blearily at the sand around her and wondered how badly she would get sunburned if she curled up right now and took a nap. But then the door opened again, and her angel beckoned to her, reaching out a hand to help her up the steps. She took his hand in hers, and let him pull her in.

Inside, it was dim, and so cool that the air felt damp. It took a moment for her eyes to adjust after the midday sun blazed down on her just minutes before. The door opened into a large, circular room, pierced in the middle by a spiraling stone staircase. It was surprisingly luxurious. A dark blue carpet covered the floor, and thickly embroidered tapestries hung all along the walls. A small, carved wooden table stood next to the door, as though the angel would have a set of car keys to set down. Bea could see doors set into the stone along the far side of the curved wall, but every one was shut, and the angel was pulling on her hand, leading her up the stairs.

They went cautiously; her steps were slow on the stone, her feet bare and blistered, her gait unsteady. The angel was patient, walking backward to watch her as she came. Bea knew that he could have carried her, if he wished, but was glad that he didn't. She could do it . . . she just needed time. They passed other floors as they spiraled upward, but Bea's eyes were fastened on her feet's painful progress, and she did not look around her as they went. It was only when they reached the top and finally stopped climbing that she looked up.

The room was beautiful. Deep red carpets covered every inch of the floor. Richly embroidered cushions lay in piles in every corner. Half the wall was made of windows, which opened to the east and made you think the whole world was perfectly blue water, stretching peacefully out to the ends of the earth. The other half was lined with books piled high on wooden bookshelves built deep into the wall. There was a tray waiting, perched on a low table on the floor. Bea sat down beside it on the rug, which was as soft as a bed. The angel pushed the table closer to her and nodded encouragingly.

There was bread, and a thick paste to spread on it that reminded her of hummus but wasn't. There were bowls of sliced fruit and olives. There were two rough clay mugs, one filled with water, the other with wine. Bea sipped from both of them gratefully. The water was clear and cold, the wine deep red and strong. The angel smiled as he, too, picked up the mug of wine, lifting it up toward her and bowing his head slightly before he took a sip. They ate in silence together, sharing the same plate, sipping from the same goblets. They did not touch or speak, but there was something so quietly powerful about the way they shared that meal. Bea did not feel at all surprised when they were finished, her angel came and lay down on the piled pillows beside her, pulling her down to him, curling tight against her back. Their legs tangled together, and she could feel the rough bristle of his chin against her scalp. She didn't mind. One of his arms draped over her, the other was a pillow for her head. She could feel him pressing close against her, and it occurred to her that if she weren't so very, very tired, she could think of any number of things she'd rather do than sleep. But her eyes were heavy, and her body refused to move. She only had time to register a deep, piercing feeling of contentment before she sank into sleep.

When she woke up, Bea was covered in the softest blanket she had ever felt. She lay long minutes, holding it against her, keeping her eyes closed, relishing the sun, warm, against her face. But she did not look.

Had she died? Had she been dreaming?

She refused to care, refused to wonder. She was warm and surrounded by softness. Her body didn't hurt.

"Enough," she thought. "Let this be enough. Let me die now, peaceful and happy. Let me die before I want again. Let this moment stretch out and on. Let this be my eternity."

He had looked at her, and his eyes had been full of something her mind was afraid to name. He had pulled her so close, and they had fit so easily together. So easy, the way his hand slipped under her head, the way her legs wrapped up and curled tight around his waist.

"Please God," she thought, praying for the first time since they had found the tumors, since everything had happened. "Please let me slip away, now, before I find something that it will rip my heart to pieces to lose. Before *I* get ripped to shreds. Again. Please. Let it happen now."

But death still would not come.

She opened her eyes, and he was there, sitting across the room from her, exactly as beautiful and perfect and horribly wonderful as he had been before. He was leaning against the wall, pillows piled high behind him, reading. But the moment her eyes opened, he set the book aside and sat up straighter, smiling at her. Bea smiled back, but her smile was laced with sorrow.

She held the blanket against her skin, suddenly self-conscious of her nakedness. The angel smiled, somehow seeming to understand exactly what she was thinking. He went to a small wooden chair by the doorway. Clothes were draped over them, and he handed them to Bea, watching the smile that crept onto her face as she examined them. A sleeveless tunic that fell past her hips, handspun in thick, cream-white cotton with strands of gold and silver interwoven throughout, that tied once in the front. She slipped it over her shoulders with delight – she had never worn anything so soft. A pair of loose-fitting, billowy pants, like pajamas, to pull up to her hips.

As soon as she was dressed, he pulled her toward the little table, which had been laid out with fresh food. They sat across from each other again, silent. There was bread, baked thick with nuts and raisins, thickly cut chunks of pineapple, and mango slices. Again, they drank clear water from the same earthen mug, sipped red wine from the same rough goblet. Bea did not speak.

For so long now, she had felt that she had been slowly slipping into silence. It had hurt that the world still wanted words from her. Friends and relatives would ask how she was feeling, but there are no words for how it feels to have your own body self-destructing from the inside out. Bea hated to try to find words to answer them with. She hated trying to smile while she lied. But the silence she found with her angel was smooth and soft. It asked nothing of her. It didn't expect her to put on a show, or be brave, or try to pretend everything was okay.

Bea looked into the eyes of her angel and found that there was nothing left to say.

When they had laughingly divided the last bit of bread between them, the angel stood and walked over to the window. Bea stood and padded on the chill stone floor to stand beside him. It was late morning, she thought, judging from the sun, bright but not at its full heat quite yet. There was nothing to see but sky and sun and water, and Bea leaned against the angel, not even hesitating before she wrapped her arm around his waist. He reached back, and lay his arm across her shoulders. There was no hesitation in their caress . . . it was the most natural thing in the world. Bea looked out at the beauty before her and thought that there was nothing else she ever wanted to see.

But then her angel stepped away and leaned over, pushing at the window with his hand. It swung open over the sea.

It was then that Bea realized . . . it wasn't a window at all.

It was a door. A door that opened into empty air.

He turned to her, his smile an invitation, and instantly Bea was clinging to him, laughing and screaming as he held tight to her and launched them both out into the sky. She kept her eyes open this time, refusing even to blink. Her heart was pounding, but not with fear. Her whole body filled with exhilaration and joy.

She had thought life was used up for her, and over. And now there was this!

The angel flew low and close to the water. Bea could see their reflection on the surface, could sometimes even glimpse the dark shadows of fish below. She could feel him looking at her, watching the delight in her eyes as she looked, laughing silently when she whooped and hollered and skimmed the surface of the water with her hand. The wind rushed all around them. Bea's eyes were constantly drawn to the angel's wings. They were so unbelievably powerful, beating slow and steady, filling with air like black leather sails puffed full with great bursts of wind.

He set them down on a beach of smooth white sand, ringed by tropical trees and deep shadows. The water was clear blue crystal; Bea could see the rocks along its bottom, could spot a fish here or there that darted toward the shore and then quickly fled back out to the sea. Bea quickly shed her clothes and ran splashing into the water; her angel settled himself down on the shore.

"Aren't you coming?" she hollered at him. The angel leaned back on his hands and smiled as he shook his head.

"You're crazy!" Bea yelled. "This water is amazing!"

But he just sat back and watched her. All day she went back and forth between him and the water, now sitting next to him in the sun, letting the waves kiss her toes before receding, now swimming in the waves, looking back to see him smiling out at her.

It was a day of silence and perfection, filled only with sunshine, the sound of the waves, and occasionally Bea's delighted laughter. When the clouds began to turn purple and pink, her angel gathered her in his arms and carried her back.

It occurred to her that "back" was already "home" in her mind, and she felt wonder, pain, and happiness mingle in her heart as he set her down on the stone floor.

Bea looked around the room. They had been gone all day, but it was not exactly as they had left it. A fire burned, waiting to greet them, in the stone fireplace. Blankets had been smoothed. The little wooden table was laden with fresh food.

"Someone's been here," Bea said, speaking for the first time in hours. The angel looked at her, not surprised, not trying to explain.

"Who else lives here?" she asked him, knowing he would not answer. He looked back at her, his expression guarded. She began to walk toward the rounded red door that opened out into the hallway, her hand reaching for the knob. He reached out and caught her hand in his, holding it tightly. When she looked at him, she saw something pleading in his eyes.

She studied him for a moment. Then, she understood.

He would not stop her. She could walk all through this place that had already become her home. She could throw open every door, examine every dark corner, drag all its secrets into the light. But he didn't want her to. He held her back, gently, his eyes asking her to stay. To leave the red door unopened.

Instantly, Bea dropped her hand and turned back, pulling him with her toward the meal that had been laid out for them. It delighted her that her angel had asked something of her, something she was able to give. And no mystery, no darkness down the stairs, could call to her more strongly than the chance to sit across from him, next to the fire.

They ate and then lay down together, the windows still

thrown open, letting the wind and the dark and the smell of the sea wash over them.

This night, Bea was not tired, and when he curled against her, she turned toward him, tasting the salt on his lips. He wrapped his arms around her, pressing her to him. There was an eagerness in his eyes, and a joy so sharp that it was pain.

Bea had been with other men, had made love many times before. But she had never given herself over to another person, had never thrown herself against someone so fiercely, had never thought to herself, “Anything he asked of me, I'd give it. Any price to be with him, I'd pay. Anything.” The moonlight streamed in through the open windows, and Bea and her angel made love in its light. There was pressure and pleasure, and the sound of Bea crying out in delight.

When it was over, and he was sleeping, Bea looked down at him: the smooth planes of his face, his arm still wrapped loosely around her.

It was only then that she realized she loved him. And she lay her head against his shoulder and wept.

EVIE

The gong's call echoed off the curved stone walls around them, multiplying and growing louder and louder until Evie's ears rang from the sound. A flock of disturbed birds burst from a crevice in the mountainside and spiraled up and up, toward the blue sky above them, complaining as they went. Evie stood, hardly daring to breathe as the sound grew and then slowly dwindled to nothing, leaving an eerie stillness in its wake.

Evie saw a flash of movement, far above her head.

She peered upward, narrowing her eyes, and realized there was a circular opening in the side of the rock; something that looked like a curved doorway. A form leaned out of that opening, with head and shoulders visible, and long hair hanging down, obscuring the faraway face. Then another head popped out of what had seemed to be solid rock. Then another and another, until dozens of pairs of distant eyes were staring down at her out of a vast number of openings in the rock-face that she hadn't even seen before.

Then there was a burst of air pressure. The sound of leathery wings slapping against the air.

Suddenly, the sky was full of Sirens.

For a minute, Evie forgot to feel afraid. The sight of them, huge wings spread, spiraling down toward her, was too strange—and too beautiful—to feel anything but awe.

The first one that came close enough for her to see it clearly was a female with wings the color of red wine, and wild, burgundy hair that matched the color of her wings exactly. The next had black wings like Roman, but his skin was deeply tanned, his build the slight, wiry build of a gymnast. He wore a long, thin sword strapped to his side. They hovered above the pavilion, the flap of their wings throwing bits of dirt and twigs up and into Evie's face.

There were more than Evie could count, a roiling cloud of rainbow colors and curling claws, hovering just above her head.

She threw her head back, staring, with her heart pounding, her hair flying wildly in the wind their wings created. Her eyes darted from one creature to the next. She was fascinated, eager to take in as much detail as she could, trying frantically to commit everything to memory, and at the same time, she felt her knees bend, as though her body was instinctively preparing to flee. She had read hundreds of descriptions of these creatures, had scraped every last detail she could find from old scrolls and translations of ancient documents that no longer existed any place but memory, but none of them had been quite right. Despite the danger she was in, a part of her heart swelled with the realization that no human record had ever come close to describing what she was seeing right now.

Roman moved to stand in front of her, trying to shield her behind his broad back. He signed frantically to the other Sirens, his hands cutting big, anxious slices through the air, his wings tense on either side of Evie, as though he could wrap her in them to protect her.

At least they were using sign, she thought to herself, and protecting her from the overwhelming and irreversible effects of hearing their voices. She tried to follow Roman's signs, but the system of signs the Sirens used in her presence had never been taught in any human school. She couldn't understand a word. She didn't need a translator, though, to understand the expressions of shock and outrage that spread across the Sirens' faces as they took in what Roman was saying.

Their wild eyes flashed with raw anger. Claws, already impossibly long, seemed to extend even farther from their hands.

The second that Roman's hands stilled, they turned to each other and, still hovering in the air, began to argue heatedly. Their hands flew with dizzying speed. Their wings beat faster and faster, till Evie felt like a small windstorm was swirling around her. She had to throw her hands up to shield her eyes from the sand and pebbles that flew through the air.

Then, with no warning, most of the Sirens flocking above them turned and soared away, shooting off at incredible speeds and disappearing back into the mountain. Only two remained: the woman with red wings and the black-winged male with a sword at his side.

The flap of their wings slowed, and they descended to the ground like birds of prey landing lightly, so as not to startle their prey into flight, one on either side of Evie. They towered over her, their broad wings held up in the air, their pupils dilated and black as they tilted their heads to the side and studied her.

The male reached up and wrapped his hand around Evie's arm, pulling her toward the stairs.

Roman bristled, stepping forward with his chest swelling, bringing up a hand to knock away the Siren's hold.

"It's alright," Evie told him quickly, reaching up to still his hand. With the tension that seethed in the air around them, she had no doubt that it would take very little for the situation to explode into violence. "I'm fine. I don't mind."

Roman stilled, watching her eyes closely for a minute before stepping back. He stretched his neck and flapped his wings, letting out a deep breath he must have been holding. He gave Evie a small nod, and understanding passed between him. He didn't want this to turn into a fight any more than she did.

Evie turned to the male Siren whose hand was still wrapped around her wrist. "I'll go with you," she assured him.

She saw the shock ripple across the Siren's face. He and the female exchanged looks of confusion, and they began signing again, first to each other and then turning to Roman with expressions of disbelief. Roman rolled his eyes, and with the air of someone who feels he is being forced to repeat himself endlessly, lifted his hands back into the air and began signing to them again.

Now Evie could at least guess what they were saying. She should have realized it would happen; that as soon as she spoke, the other Siren's would hear the lack in her voice. They knew more about her now than she would have chosen to tell them: that she had been born a Legacy, with a portion of their own Siren blood coursing through her veins. But they also knew that the promise of that power had never materialized. She was, as her mother had coldly explained to her, a cripple. Her genes had cheated her. The power coded deep inside her DNA had never risen to the surface. No matter what cruel methods Steele and her parents had tried to use to wake it, the power inside her refused to wake, and she stood, as weak as any full-fledged human, in the deepest heart of the Sirens' secret home.

Memories rose, unbidden and unwelcome, tumbling to the forefront of her mind. Pain rang deep inside her as she waited for the Sirens' eyes to fill with the same scorn she had become almost used to at home. She had been treated as less than trash by other Legacies. Her own parents had sold her for "breeding" to the highest bidder they could find, and not caring that the one who won her was Troy, a man well known for his cruelty. Her parents had only hoped to make up some of their losses. Perhaps Troy could sire a child from her. One that wouldn't be a cripple, and that they could take as their own.

Evie forced away the tightness in her throat. She threw back her shoulders and raised her chin. She wouldn't let her memories, or derision of these Sirens, get to her. They would look at her with scorn, now that they knew what she was. But the low opinions of others didn't change what she had to do. She had a role to play, and she knew it. There were things she knew that no one else did, pieces of an ancient puzzle that she would put together, no matter what.

Even if it cost her freedom and, eventually, her life.

But when the female Siren turned and looked back at Evie, her expression was thoughtful. Her eyes probed Evie's, as though searching for answers to a litany of questions that Evie couldn't begin to imagine.

The male's grip loosened, and his hand fell from Evie's arm.

She glanced over at him, startled, and he looked back at her. For a second, she thought she saw something almost admiring in his gaze, but the expression was gone so quickly that she couldn't really process it. Then, with an uncertain gesture, he motioned down the stairs, inviting her, rather than dragging her, down the steps.

Evie swallowed hard against a sudden catch in her throat, and nodded her agreement hastily, nearly tripping over her own feet in her hurry to move forward. They all walked, together, down the stairs and along the long, curving path.

As they got closer to the mountain's rocky inner wall, its shadow fell over her. Goosebumps rose on Evie's skin as they paced deeper into the shadow, right up to the face of the stone. Now she could see what had seemed to be mere shadows on the face of the rock were really curved doorways. Hundreds of them, spiraling up and around the sides of the hollow mountain, offering entry at every possible height so the winged Sirens could enter their home from almost any angle.

Evie and her escorts walked in, and Evie blinked, trying to adjust her eyes to the sudden, semi-darkness. The heavy air lay thick and moist on her skin. The cave smelled like mud and still water. Moss grew in long, green streaks across the stone walls. The silence there was so deep and still that Evie cringed at the sound her own feet made against the sand and gravel, the sound echoing off the walls, seeming to announce in louder and louder reverberations that a stranger had entered these forbidden realms.

A wooden walkway was built close against the cave wall, its wood stained green and gray from moss and mud. The Sirens led her to it, and they walked, single file, deeper and deeper into the darkness until Evie had to extend a hand in front of her, for fear of crashing into Roman from behind.

The walkway curved up and then down, till Evie's legs ached and her neck was wet with sweat despite the drop in the temperature. Then, slowly, the quality of the darkness changed. Evie could see Roman's wings in front of her. When she looked down, she could see her feet. They were no longer walking on the wooden walkway or on a rough mixture of sand and gravel. The ground beneath them was perfectly smooth stone. They rounded a corner, and Evie gasped.

It wasn't just the sudden light from a procession of bright burning torches lining the walls that surprised her. They had entered a beautiful corridor, carved from the stone. The ceiling above arched delicately. The walls sparkled in the torches' lights. Evie turned her head from side to side, trying to keep up with her escorts while still taking in every detail.

The walls were inlaid with hundreds—no, thousands—of pearls. Some silver or gray, others so perfectly white that they shone like diamonds, the pearls curled up and over every inch of the walls in seemingly endlessly intricate patterns. Images of octopi, of huge sea serpents, their heads raised high above the waves, sea stars with legs stretched open as they floated in endless, pearly oceans.

Every inch of the wall was a work of priceless art, and Evie felt something spark deep inside her chest, a light that was a twin of the torches flaring along the corridor walls.

The Sirens had made this place; this art was their own. They might be wild, even savage creatures, but she had been right: they weren't monsters. No monster could have made such works of intricate beauty.

Evie heard the claws clicking on stone long before she saw them, but still, as they rounded the corner and entered an expansive chamber, she was not prepared for the sheer number of Sirens that had gathered in a crowd, clearly waiting for her arrival. There were so many of them, even more than she had seen before, a churning chaos of colored wings and flashing eyes.

They had all gathered in front of a pair of towering, white stone doors.

Two armed Siren guards stood on either side of the door. Evie's heart stuttered then tripled the speed of its beat. She knew, with a stone-cold certainty, deep in her heart, that the Siren King waited on the other side of that door, and for a second her knees felt weak. Her head swam.

For good or for bad, her destiny would be decided on the other side of those doors. Chances were, that if she lived to walk back out of that room, it would be as a slave, her freedom and her will ripped from her forever.

The two Sirens who had escorted them led them up to the door, and the crowd parted around them, like a stream around a stone. The two guards reached up and began to pull the doors open.

Evie glanced up at Roman's face. His eyes were fastened on the light that streamed through the opening doors, his eyes wide, his face pale. His clawed hands trembled at his side.

Oh, that's just perfect, Evie thought to herself wryly. *My supernatural protector is scared out of his mind.*

But she couldn't blame him. She had known for a long time that there was a world of trouble headed her way. Roman had dived deep into all of this for her sake and was about to face the consequences of breaking his people's most sacred laws.

Pushing aside her fear of him, she reached over and touched him gently on the arm; smiling when he looked over at her.

"Don't worry," she told him softly, ignoring the stir that ran through the crowd behind them at the sound of her voice. "We'll be okay. We can do this."

He gave a small jerk of his head, a movement not so much of agreement, but of acknowledgment. Then the doors were opened, and Roman and Evie crossed the threshold into the King's throne room alone.

Evie blinked rapidly as the doors clanked shut behind them. The room was so bright that her eyes needed a few seconds to adjust. The huge chamber of stone-white walls illuminated from end to end with a seemingly endless array of torches. Evie's eyes swam and watered. The walls were bare, and the only thing in the room was a flight of steps, leading up to a throne that glittered as though carved from ice. The room was breathtaking, but Evie couldn't study it . . . she was too busy staring at the creature who sat above them, staring down at them with blazing eyes.

All of her childhood, she had been taught to fear the Watchers. To hate them. She had been taught that they were monsters, cold-blooded and eternally hungry. She had long suspected that those tales weren't true but, still, nothing had prepared her for this.

He was beautiful.

Piercing blue eyes set in an ancient, ageless face. Deep lines that edged his mouth, suggesting that his mouth, currently set in a cold scowl, was no stranger to laughter. Gray hair fell in soft curls just to his shoulders. Thick framed and long-legged, he sat perfectly still. Watching them. But, more than anything else, it was his wings that shook Evie to the core, making her question everything that she learned about these creatures. Because his wings were not thick black leather like Roman's, or even shimmery blue or deep red.

He had angel's wings.

Thick, soft feathers covered every inch of the wings that

stretched behind him, majestic and broad. His wings fluttered ever so slightly, the only part of him that moved.

Roman stood for a moment, frozen at Evie's side, staring up at his king. Then he crumpled, falling prostrate and pressing his face against the floor.

Evie couldn't move. Suddenly she felt terribly alone and very, very insignificant. What was she supposed to do now? She wondered, panic building inside her. She licked her lips, trying to force words to rise in her throat. She was standing in front of the Siren King. There was so much that she needed to tell him! But her voice was locked deep inside her. No words would come. She glanced over at Roman, but he couldn't help her now. He lay with his face pressed against the floor. Did the King expect her to prostrate herself? To kneel? Was she giving grave offense, just by standing in his presence? With a tremendous amount of effort, she tore her eyes away from the King and dropped her gaze to the floor. But she could not bring herself to kneel. All of her life, people had tried to control her. Troy had wanted nothing less than to own her; body and soul. Evie knew perfectly well that, almost certainly, she was only moments away from being permanently enthralled to a Siren.

She had the rest of her life to live on her knees.

She would speak her piece, would do what she had come here to do while standing on her own two feet. Determination flooded her, and Evie looked up, ready to meet the King's distant gaze.

Except that the King's gaze wasn't distant anymore.

He was standing right in front of her, mere inches of air between them.

Evie gasped and stumbled backward, thrown off balance by surprise.

A warm hand caught her arm. Steadying her. Powerful fingers curled around her chin, tugging her face up. And Evie found herself staring into the eyes of the King.

He studied her.

She felt as though he were looking down into her very core, running his eyes calmly over her most hidden parts, her most guarded secrets. She couldn't pull away. Time froze, her bones locked down. The moment stretched on and on. Evie couldn't breathe.

"There are . . . things . . . that I need to tell you," she finally managed to say. Her voice was strangely loud in the silent chamber, her voice making strange echoes against the walls. Each word that she forced from her lips took tremendous effort, as though the raw power the King was exuding created direct pressure on her nervous system. "The Legacies are doing something. Dangerous."

She saw his lips beginning to move. Desperation and panic surged in her chest.

"Wait," she cried. "Let me explain! There's a good reason why Roman brought me here today, and . . ."

"Silence," the King commanded, his voice like thunder, filling the room with its force.

Evie shied away. It had happened . . . she had heard a Siren's voice. She clenched her eyes shut, and waited for the oblivion to wash over her.

Except it did not come.

The fear gripped her and then lessened. Wonder came quickly in its wake.

"Do you understand now?" the King asked her, his voice softer than it had been. "My voice will do you no harm. I am different from the rest of my kind."

It was impossible. Evie had known her whole life what it meant to walk among the Watchers. But now she stood, having heard the King's voice . . . and she still knew herself. Numbly, Evie nodded.

Satisfied, the King turned from her. His face darkened as he walked over to stand in front of Roman's still prostrate form.

"Rise," he said after a moment of terrible silence.

Roman straightened slowly, his wings clapped firmly to his back, his eyes downcast. The moment he was on his feet, the King's hand flew out, striking him full force across the face. Roman stumbled backward. Evie saw shock on his face as blood trickled from his lip. He kept his eyes still fastened on the floor. He raised one hand and held it in front of his face, shielding himself, as though the King were the sun, shining on him too brightly.

"Wait! Please . . ." Evie cried, rushing to Roman's side, but the King brushed her protests aside.

"You deserve far worse than that," the King said, his voice low and dangerous. "And you may yet receive it. What is this folly? You have endangered us all."

Roman looked up. His meek demeanor had vanished. His eyes burned with anger.

His hands flew up, and he began signing, the air snapping between his fingers, his whole body leaning toward the King as his words poured out silently into the air.

Evie watched as the King's face flushed. He jerked his head back a little. Clearly, Roman's words were taking him by surprise, but he did not try to stop him and watched until Roman's words ran out and he stood, panting slightly, with his hands limp by his side.

The King turned his head away, his gaze rising up almost to the ceiling. When he turned back to face Roman, his face was once again an impartial mask.

"You must realize that what you just said is tantamount to treason," he said. Roman shrugged, as though he had gone so far into risky waters that he no longer cared or could be frightened by the consequences that might come on the heels of his action.

The King sighed heavily. He folded his hands in front of him, and his shoulders fell. "That doesn't necessarily mean you are wrong."

Roman's eyes widened in surprise, and he glanced over at Evie, who stared back at him, equally stunned.

"I will reflect on what you have said," the King continued, "and I will carefully consider what to do with you. Go to your chambers, and remain there until I have made a decision. You have disappointed me, Roman. There will be a reckoning. Go."

Roman glanced helplessly at Evie. "It's okay, Roman," she told him, though her mouth was dry. He had already risked so much, and the thought of how the King might respond if Roman disobeyed him now made her stomach clench painfully. "I'll be alright."

Pain and regret flashed across Roman's face, but he nodded to her and, silently, backed away. A moment later, the throne room doors closed behind him, and Evie stood alone in front of the King.

MOLLY

The metro was mostly deserted when Molly and Jake entered. They walked until they found an empty car, sitting down heavily, side by side.

Molly could feel Jake watching her, waiting for her to speak, to break the painful silence that throbbed between them. But it was several minutes before she could find her voice.

"You still want the drugs," she said finally. Her eyes flashed to Jake's face, a small part of her still hoping it wasn't true.

"Yes." There was so much resignation in his voice. His shoulders slumped. He looked away from her, staring at his own reflection in the darkened metro window.

"Then help me understand. I thought you were better." Molly turned to face him, wishing he would look at her. How could she have missed this? How could she possibly have not realized the struggle going on inside him, every moment of every day? Her voice broke. "You told me the pain went away!"

Jake grimaced. "What I told you was true. You just didn't understand." He turned to face her finally, but the defeated expression on his face hurt her heart. "I didn't want you to understand. The pain went away . . . the withdrawal, the aching in my bones . . . even the tremors." He closed his eyes and took a deep breath. "But I never stopped wanting it. Never stopped dreaming about getting high. I need it. It's still a part of me."

"No!" Molly's eyes flashed. "That isn't true. You might use drugs, Jake, but they aren't part of who you are."

"How could you know that?" A glimmer of anger lit Jake's eyes, and his voice was tinged with scorn. "I started drinking when I was fourteen. Started shooting up my first year of college. I don't know how I ever lived without it. I miss it . . . the way an amputee misses a limb. The way you miss someone you love after they die." He looked down at his hands. "I let you believe that I was better. I'm sorry for that; sorry if it made this harder."

"But why?" Molly's anger had dissolved as quickly as Jake's, and now she shook her head in confusion. "Why didn't you tell me?"

"I liked the lie." Jake shrugged. "I wished it could be true. I wish you could save me, Molly." He smiled ruefully. "I liked pretending I wasn't too fucked up for that. That there was still hope. I wanted to be close to you . . . to draw it out. I always knew it couldn't last." He reached out and lightly touched her hair. "It might be hard for you to believe, but these last few weeks have been the best weeks of my life. I got to have someone worry about me. To remember what it felt like to be cared for. I let you believe that I was better, Molly, because that hope made me so happy . . . I didn't want to watch it die. But it was a lie. I'm sorry."

Molly had turned her head away. She felt like such a fool. Such a failure. She cared so much about Jake, but she had been so blind. She should have known, probably could have known, if she'd been willing to look closer, to be more honest with herself. But the truth was so harsh. She hadn't wanted to let herself see.

"I liked the lie too, Jake," she said, her voice rough with unshed tears. "I should have realized that you were still in pain. But I let you suffer by yourself, rather than face something I didn't know how to handle."

"This isn't your fault, Molly!" Jake cried, his face paling with shock. But his words couldn't stop the tears that rose in her eyes. "Please don't cry. The blame is all mine. I'm sorry . . . so sorry. I've hurt you again, and I never meant to hurt you at all. Tell me what to do. Tell me how to make it better."

Molly grabbed both his hands, holding onto him as tightly as she could.

"Love me more," she said fiercely. "Love me more than the drugs."

"I already do," Jake answered, his expression anguished.

"Then stop using. Love me enough to be better."

There was a long silence.

"I don't know how," Jake whispered at last. "I don't think I can."

Molly's head fell onto his shoulder, and Jake lay a warm hand against her cheek. He leaned down and kissed the top of her head. She clutched his shirt, pulling him closer, lifting her mouth, wet from tears, and pressing it to his. She kissed him, lightly at first, but soon with a warmth that built to fire. Then her mouth was hard against his, her tongue pushing between his teeth, invading him, as though she could enter him and conquer him, and force all the wrong things inside him to be right. She swung her leg around so that she was kneeling on the seat, facing him with one knee on either side. His arm tightened around her waist, his hands clutching the thin fabric of her tank top, his hands sliding, warm, up her back. The train rounded a bend, and the momentum of it slammed her body tight against his. Jake moaned softly, and his fingers knotted in her hair. For a moment, Molly wondered wildly if, by pressing against him hard enough, she could push deep inside of him and fill up all the places where he was aching and empty. If there was any way that she could love him fiercely enough to make him whole.

The train pulled to a stop, and the lights flashed. They pulled apart, breathless, and they stared at each other. Molly's brown and red hair spilled into her face. Jake's chest rose and fell rapidly.

For a second, Molly felt like it was the first time that they had looked at each other with no illusions between them. No lies to soften the hard edges where they were both broken inside.

"Come?" she said, sliding off the seat and holding out her hand. It was a question, but she knew without a doubt how Jake would respond. He reached out and folded his hand into hers, standing up slowly, his shoulders bent like someone carrying a great weight.

They stepped off the train and walked together into the deepest shadows of the station. Jake's feet dragged, but with each step, Molly's pace quickened. Her mind, no longer reeling with shock, was filling quickly with questions. Questions that she needed answers to *now*. Confusion seethed, painful, in her mind.

Even more painful, was the small flicker of hope, that burned deep inside her, burning small but with so much intensity that it seared her insides.

Jake was still sick, still burdened. But she had fallen into a strange world that pulsed with magic. She was descended from the freaking *Sirens*, for fuck's sake!

Maybe she could still fix this.

She was just starting to understand her own powers. There had to be something more she could do. There was only one person who could help her. She knew where to go, and she yanked the key that she wore around her neck out impatiently, jamming it into the hidden elevator's lock and tapping her foot until the elevator doors opened with a low whine.

She practically jumped on, with Jake at her heels, and she slammed the door shut. There was no light inside the elevator, and she and Jake stood side by side in the utter darkness, their fingers barely touching, as the elevator descended deeper and deeper, deep under the ground.

Molly felt strangely alone in the darkness. Her whole body buzzed with adrenaline, with the desire to fix this, to make this better. With the dark all around her, she let her mind flit back to those times she hardly ever let herself remember. Back when she had been so frightened. When her every moment had been undercut with fear. How often had she wished that someone would come help her? How often had she wished that someone, *anyone*, would see her pain and promise that they'd help?

No one had come. Not ever. She'd had to become her own savior.

The feel of Jake's fingers against hers tingled, as though electric current was running out of her body and into his. Determination filled her. She would be that person for Jake that no one had ever been for her.

She was going to save him.

When the elevator finally jerked to a stop, Molly could hardly stand to hold still as the door slid open.

"Why don't you go back to our room, and wait for me there," she said to Jake. Her voice sounded strained, and she knew it, but the combination of desperation and hope swirling inside her was making the adrenaline rush like a drug through her veins. She ran a hand down Jake's shoulder, trying to reassure him. "I'll meet you there soon."

"Where are you going?" Jake's eyes were suddenly wary.

Molly took a deep breath. She knew that Jake didn't like Andrew much, even though he had never said the words out loud. She didn't blame him. Andrew was in a position of power and authority, and distrusting people like that was pretty much second nature to her, too. But Andrew had come through for her before.

And she sure as hell needed his help now.

"I have to see Andrew," she told him, and wasn't surprised to see the way his eyebrows climbed with concern.

"Why?"

Molly hesitated. She didn't want to lie to Jake. And she couldn't answer that question—at least not yet. Not until she really understood what was possible. She didn't want to give him false hope or to promise something that she couldn't really deliver.

Jake saw the uncertainty in her eyes. "Don't go see him, Molly. At least, not right now," he urged her. "We've both had a rough night. Come back to the room with me. You need some rest." He grimaced and lowered his voice, "And, besides. There's something . . . off about that guy."

"I know you don't like him Jake, but he knows a lot. And I need to talk to him right now."

Jake pressed his lips together stubbornly but said nothing.

"Please Jake," Molly said. "I'll be there before too long. Just go on ahead."

She was careful not to make her words an order, but still, they both know that she could have ordered him to do as she said. Suddenly, Jake seemed to deflate. The protest in his eyes flickered and died.

"Sure," he muttered. "Whatever you say. I'll see you there." He thrust his hands deep into the pockets of his jeans and spun around, walking away from her quickly, his head bent low. He didn't look back.

Molly watched him go, the emotions in her chest swirling so frantically that she couldn't even tell what she was feeling. After he rounded the corner and disappeared from sight, she straightened up and ran her fingers through her hair. Her cheeks were dry, but she ran her hands roughly over her face anyway, rubbing her eyes hard, like someone waking from deep slumber. Then she spun on her heel, and with long strides hurried down the hall to Andrew's room.

She didn't stop to wonder what time it was until after she had rapped loudly on his door. The sound echoed, and Molly cringed, suddenly realizing that it was probably close to three in the morning. There was a moment of pregnant silence, and then Molly could hear the sounds of scuffling behind the door. It might not have been the best strategy to wake Andrew in the dead of night to ask for his help, but she threw her shoulders back, determined not to quell under his gaze.

Jake was in trouble. This couldn't wait.

Still, when the door finally opened, Molly couldn't help but start in surprise. She had been expecting Andrew, but it was a woman who pulled the door open and gazed dispassionately through the crack. It took Molly a moment to remember the name of the beautiful, pale woman with long, black hair, who seemed perfectly groomed and was wearing a short, sleeveless black dress, despite the late hour.

"Can I help you?" the woman asked, her tone businesslike.

Molly fished in the back of her mind for the woman's name. "Hi Denise," she said, trying to smile. "I'm sorry to bother you so late. But I need to speak to Andrew. It's urgent."

"Hold on," Denise replied. Then she closed the door in Molly's face.

Molly was still blinking in surprise, staring at the shut door in front of her, when Denise pulled the door open a little wider and stood to the side.

"Come on in," Denise said, her voice still cold and emotionless.

Molly stepped inside. Andrew's office looked different now, lit only by the fire in the fireplace. The shadows moved erratically, dancing on the drawings of goblets and daggers that Andrew had plastered on every inch of his walls.

Molly moved to the center of the room, watching Denise out of the corner of her eye. Her sleeveless black dress plummeted at the neckline and stopped above the knee. As striking as the woman was, with thick black hair that fell to the small of her back, and a pale, perfect face, complete with smooth skin, high cheekbones, and a seemingly permanent expression of disdain, it was her bracelet that Molly's eyes were drawn to. Blood-red stones encircled her wrist, their color a shocking contrast to her fair skin.

Her bracelet was a twin of the one that Jake wore. The one that had been given to him by the other Echoes, after Molly had formed the bond between them; a bond that she was still struggling to really understand.

Denise was a Bloodbound, like Jake. Somehow, Molly had forgotten.

"Molly! What's the matter?" Andrew hurried out of one of the back rooms, still pulling on a tee shirt over his worn jeans. His red hair was tousled and slightly flattened on one side. His eyes were still a little foggy with sleep.

"I'm sorry to bother you so late." Molly felt suddenly awkward. It had felt so natural to come to Andrew for help, for guidance. But now she found herself wondering if she had overstepped herself somehow. "I really need to talk to you."

"Of course." Andrew turned to the woman. "Denise, sweetheart, why don't you give us some privacy?"

The woman nodded, the movement a little jerky. Almost unnatural. Denise didn't say anything, just stalked silently into one of the back rooms. Molly heard a door click shut behind her.

Andrew's face was full of concern as he reached out and pulled Molly all the way into the room, sitting down on one of the couches. Molly sank into the cushions, and let her head fall into her hands.

"What happened?" he asked gently. "Tell me everything."

And Molly did. The events of the night poured from her lips, and the more she talked, the more sure she felt that Andrew could help her. He nodded when she told him the way that her voice had failed to work on Janice, as though things that mystified her made complete sense to him. He listened intently as she explained everything that she had learned from Jake. Andrew listened without comment, his eyes never straying from her face, giving an encouraging nod now and then, if her words seemed to slow.

"I need you to train me," she told him, finally, when her story was done. "I have to learn how to use my abilities more fully. That's got to be the problem, right? I'm still new to all of this.

That's why I couldn't tell Janice not to feel afraid, and I haven't been able to make Jake stop wanting the drugs. You can help me fix that." She said it with such confidence. But then she looked at the expression on Andrew's face, and her heart sank. "Right?"

Andrew leaned back and sighed heavily.

"I'm sorry," he said after a short silence.

"What does that mean?" Molly demanded. She could feel all the desperation inside her, poised and ready to turn into anger. With tremendous effort, she swallowed the emotion down. Yelling at Andrew wouldn't help Jake. "You said that I'm one of the most powerful Echoes you've ever seen. I just need to fix Jake's addiction. That's all. If I'm as powerful as you say, then I ought to be able to do that!"

"It isn't that simple, Molly," Andrew said. He reached out to take her hand in his, but Molly pulled back. She didn't want sympathy or hand-holding. She wanted to understand.

"Why?" she asked through clenched teeth. "It seems pretty simple to me."

"I know it does." Andrew leaned toward her, resting his elbows on his knees. "And you've come so far in so little time, that sometimes I forget there are things, basic things, that you still haven't learned." He chuckled a little to himself, a short, bitter sound. "You've known from the first day we met that I've been searching my whole life for this goblet," he flicked a hand toward all the drawings of the goblet that lined his walls. "But all this time, you never really understood why. I'm sorry that I didn't explain things to you earlier."

"Well, I'm listening now," Molly prodded. She didn't want apologies. She wanted to make Jake better. Now.

"There is a fundamental difference between our power and the power of full-blooded Sirens." Andrew shrugged. "Maybe it's better this way. For you to learn for yourself so that you could really understand why things have to change." He leaned in closer to her. "We have only half the power that we ought to have. As

Echoes, the power of our voices is limited to physical control. We can make a person's body do anything we want . . . if the speaker's voice is strong enough, it will happen. But that is where our power ends. When it comes to emotions, our abilities hit a brick wall. We can make a person *do* things, but we can never control how they *feel* about doing them. Or, in Jake's case, you can physically stop him from taking the drugs. But you can't uproot the craving that he has for them."

Molly shook her head. "You're saying that I can't help him," she said, and now she let the anger that had been stirring inside her leak into her voice. "I can't accept that. I won't."

"And you shouldn't." Andrew nodded, the fierceness in his voice rising to match the anger in Molly's. "It isn't right. We've been denied our birthright for too long. The Watchers are jealous guardians of a power that they refuse to even make use of. They leave us to be slaughtered by the Legacies, refusing to step in and stop the violence. And yet, at the same time, refusing to grant us access to the one thing that would make us safe forever." He pointed at the drawings of the goblet again, and for the first time, Molly really looked at the image that Andrew was so clearly obsessed with. The goblet didn't look like much: pale white stone, no discernible markings.

"You're saying that, somehow, the goblet could change that?"

Andrew nodded. "The goblet couldn't give just anyone power. If a regular human were to drink out of it, it would destroy them. But for us—for anyone with a trace of Siren blood running in their veins who drinks from that goblet . . ." For a moment, words seemed to fail him. He leaned back against the cushions, exhaling a heavy breath. "It would make our voices just as powerful as a full-blooded Siren's. Just as powerful, Molly! Imagine that! If just a few of us were that strong, it would change everything. We would be able to fight them. Really fight them. We'd be able to throw off their yoke, once and for all. We'd be able to truly fight back against the Legacies." He looked at Molly, and his eyes gleamed. "You could cure Jake. With a single sentence."

Molly swallowed, her mouth suddenly dry.

"You're sure?" she asked. She wanted him to promise her, to swear right then and there that it was really possible. That she could really make Jake be okay.

Andrew's face lit up. "Don't you understand what I'm trying to tell you? The Sirens can do what we can't . . . their voices have power over more than the physical. Their voices go right to the core . . . to the soul, the heart. It *is* possible, Molly. And we are very, very close."

For a long moment, Molly stared at Andrew. She wanted to believe what he was saying. And there was no risk that she wouldn't take for Jake.

"Then why are we waiting?" she asked, pretending that her stomach wasn't twisting with nerves and that the tips of her fingers hadn't gone cold. "Let's go get it."

Andrew shook his head. "It isn't so easy. Thanks to Evie, we at least know where it's hidden. But the Sirens have it heavily guarded. According to Evie's research, each Siren has to 'donate' one of his human servants . . . the strongest and fiercest one, to stand constant guard around the goblet. There are hundreds of them."

Molly nodded slowly to herself. One by one, the pieces started to come together in her mind. "That's why you were so excited when you learned that my voice can control whole groups of people at once.You need me to get past the guards."

"It's a very rare gift," Andrew agreed. "And I think your ability is the key in the lock that will get us to the goblet. The Sirens are used to going unchallenged," Andrew went on "They've held all of the households, through fear and intimidation, for generations. It is probably unthinkable to them that we would try to resist them now. Their over-confidence makes them weak. All we need is that goblet. And the longer we wait, the greater the risk that Steele will get there first. And you don't even want to imagine what will happen, to all of us, if Steele manages to get that kind of power." Andrew leaned in closer to Molly, his breath warm on her cheek. "But we need you," he said, his voice urgent. "We need your voice to get us past the guards."

Molly's heart beat so quickly that she could hear its beating faintly in her ears.

"And if we get it, I can cure Jake?" she asked, needing to hear the words again.

Andrew smiled at her, and the warmth of his expression was like the sun rising.

"Yes," he promised, without a moment's hesitation. "He'll never want drugs again."

Molly's heart swelled.

"Then what are we waiting for?" she asked, her hands balling into fists on her knees. "Let's got get the goblet."

Andrew grinned at her, his expression almost child-like in its pure excitement. "Okay." Andrew sat up a little straighter and ran a hand through his rumpled hair. "I have to contact someone. He's a partner of sorts. He's the one who first told me about the goblet, and he's been helping me to search for it all these years. He'll want to come with us. And then . . ." Andrew took a deep breath. "We'll go after the goblet. Together."

"Give me a day or two to get everything ready," Andrew told her, standing.

"Okay." Molly was glad her voice sounded steady, and she rose, too.

Andrew walked her to the door. Patting her on the shoulder, he softly closed the door behind her.

But not before Molly caught a glimpse of the wild triumph on his face.

EVIE

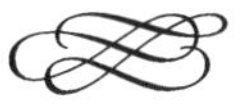

Evie and the King stared at each other in silence.

The King flicked his wings and settled them behind his back. He leaned his head to the side, stretching his neck.

"Roman says we have failed you," he said, the words clipped by annoyance. Evie said nothing, stunned that Roman thought that. That he had dared to say such a thing to his king. She had never said a word of reproach to Roman. It was true that Roman frightened her, but she didn't blame him for the lies he had told her or the decisions he had made. He had risked everything to try to help her. She was pretty sure that she knew who her monsters were, and between Troy and her parents, she had more than enough already.

She said nothing. The King narrowed his eyes.

"What are you?" the King demanded. "You are not human. But I hear no power in your voice."

Evie blinked. This conversation had taken a turn she never expected it to take.

"I came to warn you," she said, finally finding her voice. "The Legacies . . ."

But the King cut her words off with a sharp shake of his head.

"I rule here! I will ask the questions, and you will answer them," he thundered, and despite herself, Evie took a step back, away from him. "What are you?"

"I . . . I'm Evie," she stammered. "My parents are Legacies. But the power never came to me."

The King grimaced. "And what fault of mine could that possibly be?" he asked, his voice an outraged rumble. But something about Evie's expression made him still. He watched her closely for a moment and then stepped closer. His voice dropped. Gentled. "What has happened to you, child?"

Evie felt the blood drain from her face. She felt suddenly as though the walls of the room were closing in around her, boxing her in. Her breath came faster, but she couldn't quite fill her lungs.

Without even knowing that she did it, she shook her head once in a quick, desperate motion of refusal.

"I must know," the King insisted. When Evie's silence stretched on, his face darkened. "I will know the truth," he told her. "Every bit of it. One way or another."

The threat hung in the air between them. Either Evie would tell him of her own free will, or he would strip her freedom from her, and take the truth from her that way.

She had no choice. But still, forcing the words out was almost impossible. She didn't talk about it. Had never talked about it except for once, in a place where she felt safe, to someone she felt sure would understand. Now she felt as though the mere act of parting her lips would rip the barely healed wounds wide open. She hung her head. Clenched her eyes shut, as though she could speak of the memories, but still somehow hold them outside of her mind. Keep them at a distance.

The words were halting. Slow. She told the King about how her parents had taken her to Steele for "treatment," to try to force her voice to surface. The pain. The experiments. The way she begged them to stop, while secretly hoping that something that he did to her, no matter how painful, would work. So that she could have her family back again. She told him about how, when nothing worked, and it became clear that she would always be a "cripple," Steele suggested they sell her for breeding.

The words choked her as she spoke, and her eyes were still clamped shut, but she wasn't sure she could have stopped the tears from flowing at this point, even if she wanted. She felt as though she was reliving everything that had happened, as though she were back in her room, at this very moment. Waking up, in the same bed where her mother had tucked her in and wished her sweet dreams every night, to Troy standing over her. She could almost hear his voice now, telling her that he wanted to "sample the goods he'd paid for." She could hear the screams that ripped from her throat, the cries for help to her parents, just down the hall. They could hear her screaming

But no one came.

She didn't cry when she was done talking. She felt tired and empty. She stood, her hands limp at her side, and opened her eyes slowly. Maybe she should have just let the King take her freedom. Maybe then telling the story wouldn't have hurt her quite so much.

It took her a second to realize that the King was no longer standing over her. He had backed away and sat down on the steps leading up to his throne. He looked strangely vulnerable sitting there, with his fine robes dragging on the ground, and a hand resting over his mouth.

He didn't speak to her, but stood and walked swiftly to the door of his throne room. He pulled the door open a crack and spoke to the sentry standing outside.

"Go to Roman's chambers immediately," he ordered the guard. "Tell him that he is released from house arrest." He turned, his eyes locking with Evie, "He is more in the right than I am."

He closed the door and, his steps slow, went back to sit on the steps again. Then he motioned to the spot beside him, inviting Evie to join him.

Moving slowly, and feeling as though she were dreaming, Evie went and sat beside the Siren King.

"Roman was right," the King said, his lips quirking, as though the words left a bitter taste on his tongue. "We have failed you. It has been many generations since we ruled the Legacy households as we should. And now you say that they are mounting some kind of rebellion against us?"

"They have learned of the moonstone goblet," Evie told him. "And Steele is determined to find it and use it for himself."

The King shook his head. "That's impossible!" he cried, and for a second Evie mistook the emotion in his eyes for anger. But then his face paled, and she realized, with a tremor of shock that rolled through her whole body, that the Siren King was afraid.

"We've done everything possible to destroy all knowledge of that goblet!" The King protested. Evie shifted uneasily and decided not to tell him that she herself had done a great deal of the research that had brought the goblet's existence to light. "The threat that it poses to our survival is so great that we would have destroyed it generations ago if we had not feared bringing our Mother's wrath down on us and worsening our curse!"

"Wait a minute, what do you mean?" Evie asked, narrowing her eyes. "I came to warn you because I know Steele. If he became more powerful, he could do even more terrible things than he has already done."

"You do not know, then, where the goblet gets its power? Or what the liquid is that it contains?"

"No," Evie answered, shaking her head. "And I don't know what curse you are talking about, either."

"My people were born at the very beginning of this world," he said. "Back when the Creator formed the two great lights, ordering the sun to rule the day, and the moon to rule the night. This much you know?"

Evie nodded mutely. Everyone knew that story.

"What you do not know is that the sun and moon were not

always as you see them now. At first, the sun and the moon were equal in strength. They shone with equal brightness, and the world did not know darkness or fear. But the sun and the moon argued. Of this, there is some whisper still among mankind. Ancient Jewish Midrashim tell of how the sun and the moon argued before God, each wishing to gain dominion over the other. The moon lost the argument. And then she was reduced, in both her size and her brightness. She became so weak that she could no longer hold the dark at bay.

"In the darkness of her absence, evil was born into the world. She had been commanded to rule the night, but now she was too weak. She loved the humans far below her and grieved for the evil that befell them in the darkness. Humans turned on each other, once their faces were hidden. Other creatures, too, grew bolder. They found humans were easy prey.

"The moon wept and filled the oceans of the world with the salt water of her tears. Out of her grief, she bore children." The King motioned to himself. "The Watchers. She clothed us in wings of white and gifted us with voices as pure and piercing as a moonbeam. She sent us down to be her Watchers in the night, to keep the peace for her on nights when her own light waned. Men called us angels." The King shook his head. "And for a time we walked among them. Beloved. Honored. At that time all of us wore feathers, and each possessed two voices; a human voice and a heavenly one. We could converse safely with humans if we so chose. Only to stop violence were we to use our other voices; even then, they were meant to be merciful, preserving the life of the guilty, turning them from lives of depravity to usefulness. We were not wholly evil. But the temptation was too great.

"Of this, too, there is record, though much has been misunderstood. The purest is in Genesis, where it is written, 'The Neflim saw that the daughters of man were beautiful, and they took for themselves wives from whomever they chose.'"

"Neflim?" Evie asked, interrupting for the first time. "I've heard that word before. I can't remember what it meant."

"Most do not translate it correctly. They believe the word comes from the word 'nefal' meaning fallen. They took us for fallen angels, descending to earth to cavort with human women." The King snorted derisively. "Our name always meant 'Overseers,' much the same as how we are known to your kind today."

"As the Watchers."

"Yes. Historically, we are condemned for fathering half-human children."

"You mean us?" Evie lay her hand against her chest. "The Legacies?"

The King nodded. "Yes, and the Echoes as well. They are equally our children. At the time, we did not stop to think about the shadow of our own power that we would pass on to our partly human descendants. We did not consider what harm might be done. But fathering the Echo people was hardly the worst thing we did."

Evie held her breath, watching as the King closed his eyes and bowed his head.

"We enslaved entire towns," he said softly. "Drunk on the power of our voices to enthrall anyone who might stand in our way, we did not hold back our hands from any good thing. There was no one to stop us.

"We forgot that our Mother was watching . . . but she was. And her anger burned hot against us. She created the moonstone goblet, to weaken us and to strengthen the one she chose to carry out her judgment. She created the moonstone knife, to carry out the sentence she pronounced. In one bloodstained night, every Siren who had spilled human blood was killed; their throats slit with a moonstone knife until the sand ran red beneath our feet. The rest were cursed; our human voices ripped away, our feathers stripped from our wings. So that we appeared the monsters that we had become. Now the slightest sound of our voices would rip any humans will away forever, no matter how we tried to prevent it. And we know that to take a human's life needlessly would bring down our Mother's rage on us again. So we made homes for ourselves on the edges of the water, and only rarely did any humans glimpse us. When they did, they did not understand. Myths sprang up around us. Once they had called us angels, but after that night the humans thought us demons. Sirens."

"You speak of it as though you were there," Evie said softly.

The King shook his head. "Our lives are longer than humans', but I am not so ancient. Still, I have relived it many times, in dreams. As king, I am exempt from the curses that plague our kind. Of all our people, only I can converse with you safely. And only I still bear my feathers. But I carry my own burden."

The King smiled bitterly, as he answered the unspoken question in Evie's eyes.

"Prophecy," he explained. "Our Mother sends me visions, both of what was and of what may be." He smiled slightly. "Though I do not know what answer you will give me now."

"Answer?" Evie's mouth was dry. "To what?"

"To my proposal." The King stood up, and his tone became businesslike. "You must realize, Evie, that we cannot simply send you back. Though you have committed no crime, you know too much about us. You have seen our home. We cannot allow you to leave with this knowledge, so, only two paths remain. You could bind yourself to one of us."

"I don't want to be a slave!" Evie cried, jumping to her feet as adrenaline flooded her system.

"Stop and think before you say that, Evie." The King's voice was soothing. "You would be happy . . . happier than you have ever been. You have suffered. You are scarred. We can wipe all that away. I would give my own daughter, Nomi, as your Singer. She is a kind child and would be a good companion for you. All that you have endured . . . the fear, the betrayal. The deprivation. It would be less than a dream to you."

"My scars are nothing to be ashamed of," Evie said, her eyes burning. "You carry a burden, and so do I. I am strong enough to bear it."

"There is another way." The King's eyes were pushing into her.

"What?" Evie asked, wary. She could tell from the King's expression that even he was not sure that she would want what he offered.

"Join us," he said simply. "Become one of us. Share in our power, and in our burden." He smiled regretfully. "Sadly, I cannot give you one without the other."

"Is that even possible?" Evie gasped.

"It is," the King said steadily. "You are an Echo. Our blood, though diluted, already runs in your veins. A full human could never join our ranks, but one who shares our blood. . ."

"But I have no power, no voice!" Evie protested. "Even among the Legacies, I was considered a weakling!"

"I assure you, it makes no difference." The King said, taking a step toward her to close the distance between them. "You are of our blood, Evie. If you choose, you may become one of us fully. I do not offer this lightly. It has only been done a handful of times in our long history. But you have shown great strength, and what Roman told me was true: we have failed you. We should have protected you, and we did not. We owe you a debt. I cannot give you back what has been taken from you. But I can offer you a new life. You would be accepted and treasured among us. Your knowledge of the human world, of the Legacy and Echo households . . ." The King raised his hands expressively. "Here they would be considered rare gifts. There is a war coming. I have need of the things that you know. You need feel no loyalty to your parents, to the ones who raised you and then treated you as less than garbage. If you choose to stand with us, I can make you stronger and more powerful than you have ever been."

"And if I refuse?"

The King looked at her sadly. "Then I will call my daughter," he said gently. "And she will sing to you."

"No," Evie cried, the words rushing out almost instantly. "I'll join you." She felt not the slightest bit of hesitation. She clung to the King's offer like a drowning man clutching at a raft.

The King nodded, but his expression didn't change.

"You knew that, didn't you?" she asked. "All this time that we've been talking, you knew what you would offer me, and how I would answer. That's why you have told me all of these things."

The King smiled faintly. Then he clapped his hands once.

The door to the throne room flew open. The female Siren with red hair, who had escorted Evie here, stood in the doorway, an ornate cup in her hands. It steamed and bubbled. She walked toward the King and handed the cup to him, and then glided backward swiftly, without so much as glancing at Evie's face. The door swung shut silently behind her.

"That isn't . . ." Evie gasped, staring at the cup. "The moonstone goblet?"

The King shook his head. "No," he said, his face serious. "This is something else."

"What is it?" Evie asked, but the King shook his head.

"Enough questions!" the King snapped, his expression hardening. "You must drink the contents of this cup. All of it."

"And it will make me change?" Evie asked, trying to keep her voice from trembling.

"Not yet. This will prepare your body, and open your mind. It will give you a vision, one that we must share together. It is the only way for us to know if the path you have chosen is the way that your life is truly meant to be. Only after you have tasted the water, and seen what it has shown you . . . only then will you be ready to undergo the change."

Without another word of explanation, the King raised the goblet to eye level. He looked at it steadily, whispering to himself inaudibly before bringing it to his lips. He took only the smallest of sips, barely concealing a grimace when he tasted it. He handed the steaming goblet to Evie, who hurried to tip it down her throat before she could stop to think of what she was doing.

It tasted like hot rot, and cinnamon.

Evie gagged as she swallowed, letting the cup fall from her fingers and clang against the floor when she was done.

She turned to the King, who was watching her expectantly. For one, long, thrilling moment, she met his eyes, full of defiance. Then it hit her, the pain like an expanding balloon swelling in her gut. Her heart pushed up and into the wall of her chest, beating frantically, like a bird breaking its wings against the bars of a cage. She sat down heavily on the floor, cross-legged, holding her head up with her hands. Colors popped in front of her eyes, lilacs and delicate blues. She gasped for breath, and it came slowly, unwillingly, pulling itself sluggishly down her throat to where her lungs were burning.

"What's happening to me?" she moaned.

The King squatted beside her, his hand on her shoulder, keeping her from tipping over.

"The worst will pass in a moment," he said, his voice barely audible above the ringing in her ears; but he was right. In the same instant that he stopped speaking, the pain quieted, like some ravenous beast that froze mid-stride, muscles quivering. She knew it wasn't gone, knew it still crouched, deadly, inside her. But for the moment, she didn't care. The pain had stopped.

She looked down at her arms. It was only then that she realized she was holding a baby.

A tiny head. Soft brown downy hair, the color of coffee with cream, covered it thickly, sticking up in awkward places. A warm body, unbelievably tiny, and yet somehow so incredibly alive, squirming faintly against her. Eyelids that opened only a sliver before squeezing shut, allowing her the briefest glimpse of the cinnamon brown eyes beneath them. A pink perfection of minuscule lips, forming a tiny O as they nestled against her, bumping against her breast.

"What?" Evie tried to say, but the word was lost in a cry of delight.

"Your daughter," the King said, though Evie had forgotten him. She had forgotten nearly everything. "Ariella."

"Ariella! Yes, of course. I know. I know her!" Evie ran her fingers reverentially across the soft hair. She leaned down low and ran her nose against her daughter's arm, the soft baby skin warm against hers. She breathed deeply of her daughter's smell. She pressed her, tight but gentle, against her breast. She felt a stinging tingle in her nipples, and milk leaked from her, dribbling down her stomach, staining the front of her shirt.

Everything she had ever wanted, she now held in her arms.

Beauty. Innocence. Love effortlessly given and unquestioningly returned.

All the love Evie had but had not been able to give away, that she had stored up and locked away deep inside, till it turned toxic and poisoned her from within . . . all of it poured out of her now. It wrapped around that little child, latching onto her forever. Evie leaned down and buried her face in the soft perfection of her baby. She closed her eyes, and let the tears of joy run down her face.

The King sighed, the sound deep and full of pain. Evie opened her eyes and looked up at him wonderingly. He met her eyes, and she was shocked to see his perfect blue eyes lined with red. Unshed tears sparkled from his eyes.

She looked down. The child was gone.

"A vision of the future, Evie," the King said quickly, his voice strangely strained. "A vision of the child that may yet come to be."

"May?" The word was strangled with all the grief that crashed inside her heart.

"You have seen her. You know her name. Now you must be wary. Prophecy is a gift that comes with a heavy cost. Your knowledge of her is a threat to her ever coming into existence. She is fragile . . . her future is still uncertain. You must lock all that you know of her deep inside yourself. If you speak of her . . . if you say her name . . . if you try to bring the reality of her existence into the world before her time is right . . . you will shatter your vision, and it will never come to be. You must be very cautious. Do you understand?"

"Why show me, if it puts her in danger?" For the first time Evie was angry with the King; for the first time, she raised her voice to him.

"I do not control the vision, Evie. I merely shared it. Prophecy cannot be forced on anyone— you had to accept it willingly. If I had poured the potion down your throat, the vision would have flown from you. It had to happen this way."

His words confused, and for some reason, frightened her. Or perhaps it was not his words, but the coldness that crept into them as he was speaking, the way he rose and turned his back to her before his words were done.

But whatever it was that unsettled her, Evie was distracted. A door swung open. She had not noticed it before. It was wooden, hidden in a shadowy back corner of the room.

"What . . ." she started to ask, but the King interrupted her, though he did not turn to look her in the face.

"For you," he said coldly. "You must walk through."

Evie looked at his back questioningly, but he did not speak again, and he did not turn. She pushed herself to her feet. He was right. She felt a need to walk through the door, felt it calling to her. There was something terrible, and inevitable, about it. She was across the room before she even realized that she had moved her feet, crossing the threshold and entering into a room full of sickly, yellow light. The door swung shut behind her.

"Hi, sweetheart," Troy said. "I've been waiting for you."

EVIE

Every cold night of terror, every moment of panic she had ever had—this moment was worse than them all.

"You can't be here," Evie said numbly.

"Of course I'm here, honey. We've been searching the whole fucking world for you, haven't they?" Troy smiled at her broadly.

She took a bewildered step back. The door was shut tight behind her back. The room was dimly lit, but she didn't need bright lights to see Troy's face clearly. He leered down at her every night in her nightmares.

"No," she said, trying to sound sure. "No. Roman brought me here so that I could see the King."

"That's what they wanted you to believe. You made it clear that you were more than willing to kill yourself to get away, so we had to be real careful. The Watchers had to keep you calm. Controlled. They had to tell you a story you could believe in, while they got the information that they wanted out of you. And I had to wait till they were through with you so that I could have my turn." He stepped forward, and caught a lock of her hair in his fingers, pulling on it experimentally, as though testing its springiness between his fingers. Evie wanted to run, to scream. To kick and punch and fight to get away. But her whole body was locked down. A cold wave of shock ran through her. Her feet wouldn't move.

"They knew I wouldn't want them to break you," Troy went on. "Not when I've been looking forward to doing it myself for so very long. You're mine now. Did you think you could just run away like that? After the deal had been struck? After your idiot parents had taken my money?" He smiled. His voice dropped. "After I tasted you? I've owned you ever since that night."

"No," Evie gasped, the air burning her throat. "You're wrong. You're lying!" her voice climbed closer to a scream. "It doesn't make any sense. The Sirens would never help you!"

"Are you kidding?" Troy gave a dry, mirthless chuckle. "You've been working with the Echoes. Helping them pry secrets they have no business knowing out of the past. You're a threat to them."

"I just wanted to stop you!" Evie moaned. Her heart pounded at breakneck speed, and she closed her eyes. She couldn't let herself faint. God knows what he'd be doing to her when she woke up. "I haven't broken any rules."

"Sure you have. You're a fucking criminal." His voice rose, and his lips pulled back from his teeth. "You think you can just choose where you go?" he snarled. "You're a Legacy. You belong to us. It doesn't matter if you're a cripple. That doesn't get you a free pass. You've got the genes in you. You've got a goddamned fucking gold-mine right there between your legs! You don't get to run away . . . you've got to breed me a son."

"No," Evie said again. "The King told me. . ."

"The King and I have been real tight for a long time. Check and see, Evie. He locked the door behind you."

It was true. Evie turned and tore at the knob, but it wouldn't open.

"No!" she shouted and pounded on it. "NO! Help me! PLEASE!"

She didn't see him come up behind her, but he grabbed her savagely by the hair and threw her to the floor. He rolled her onto her back, and she was bewildered by how much it hurt when he knelt on top of her. He knelt with his knees resting just above her elbows, his full weight pinning her arms to the ground. After just a minute, she could hardly feel her fingers anymore. She thrashed and struggled, kicking with her feet. She screamed and fought till sweat poured down her face and her screams had turned to sobs. He held her down, watching her. Enjoying her struggle. She could feel him, hard, pressing into her chest. She didn't see him reach behind and pull the knife from his belt, but she froze when he held it in front of her eyes.

"You might want to hold still now, Evie," he said softly, pressing the knife against her cheek. "If you don't, I might do more than just mark you."

He pulled the knife across her skin, slow, his tongue sticking out beneath his teeth, his brows drawn, pulling the blade in a long line from the edge of her temple, all the way down her cheek.

Evie screamed and screamed. Troy didn't even seem to notice.

She could feel the blood trickling, hot and thick, down her neck. It was the feel of it, that soft, wet drip, that made her lose control. A haze of panic descended. She could feel herself from a distance: the way her body spasmed, the curses that spilled, useless, from her lips.

Troy smiled, and slowly repeated the cut on the other side of her face.

"Something to remind you," he murmured as he worked. "From now on. Every time you look in the mirror . . . you'll remember who owns you." He leaned in close to her face, letting the stubble on his chin scrape her chin. "You've been mine since that night. Now you'll be mine completely. You'll never defy me again, Evie. Never. Tonight you'll learn that lesson. You'll pay the price for what you've done. Now. Tell me. What is the name you heard in your dream?"

"Wh . . . what?"

"The name. Say it."

"I don't understand," Evie had stopped crying. She stared at him. "But the King said . . ."

Troy slapped her, hard, across her bloody cheek.

"I know what he fucking said; I was listening the whole time!" Troy shouted. "I don't want a daughter! I want a son! Wasn't that the point of this whole fucking charade? Say the name, Evie. Kill the girl before she lives. She isn't what I bought you for. Say it. You know you have to."

He pressed the blade against her throat.

Could it be true? Could that beautiful angel she saw in her dream really be this monster's spawn? Evie closed her eyes and felt the tears roll down the sides of her face, stinging in her wounds, pooling on the ground under her.

A child of rape.

Born of her slavery to this man she hated. Could it be? The image of her baby rose before her eyes, the soft head, the downy hair, the mouth that opened into a tiny pink O and turned toward her, needing her. Loving her.

And then Evie knew it didn't matter. It didn't matter where she came from. Evie's parents, the parents she had loved, and adored, and tried her whole life long to please . . . they were monsters, too. She *loved* that child. She needed to love her. Needed to finally, for once in her life, give love to someone who actually deserved to receive it. That love was the only thing that mattered to her in the world.

"No," she said, opening her eyes. "I never will."

"Sure you will," Troy whispered. "You'll do any goddamned thing I tell you. And if you don't, I'll kill you right now."

He pressed the blade, hard against her throat and leaned down over her, leering.

"If you kill me, I'll never give you any children," Evie gasped.

Troy's face turned red. He pressed the blade against her so

deeply that she felt it break the skin. "I can have any woman I want," he grunted throatily. "No one runs away from me and lives. I had to find you. I had to prove that. And I have. If you won't give me what I want now, I'll kill you and find someone who will. Tell me, Evie! Say the name now!"

Evie closed her eyes. She wouldn't let this man be the last thing she ever saw. She closed her eyes and remembered the dream of her daughter. The smell of her.

"No," she whispered, and in her mind, she held her baby tight against her.

"Tell me!" Troy screamed, but it was as though he yelled at her from a great distance.

Evie didn't even bother to refuse. There was a silence inside her. It had grown slowly, over all those long months of walking through crowds where no one knew her name, through the years of hiding. She found it now and wrapped it like a shield around herself. She would not speak. She did not even open her eyes to see him raise the knife, did not know it was arcing toward her till she felt its bite against her skin. Her lips did not move, but in her heart, she cried out.

"Ariella!" she screamed, in the deepest, most secret part of her soul.

And then she woke.

The King's arms were tight around her shoulders, holding her up. She lay in a tight ball at the foot of the throne room steps. She was shaking and tear-stained. Her clothes were soaked with sweat and clung to her skin.

She was not hurt.

Her fingers flew to her neck, then to her face. No blood. Nothing but tears and shaking that would not stop.

"You're alright," the King murmured. "It was only a vision."

Evie pushed away his hands and turned her head to the side. She vomited clear water, and then crouched, hands flat against the cold stone, panting.

"You had to prove yourself before we could allow you to join us," the King explained. "Before we could trust you to guard the power that we all hold. You had to show that you could control yourself. You had to prove that you had the silence within you. Not many do."

Evie turned to the King.

"That was a cruel, cruel test," she whispered hoarsely. The King nodded.

"Yes," he admitted. "And it is a cruel power you lay claim to. I had to be sure."

Evie wiped tears from her cheek. "And my daughter?" she asked, trembling inside. "Was she real?"

"Yes," the King answered. "I, too, have seen her."

"Is she safe?" Evie asked anxiously. "Will she still come to be?"

The King nodded slowly. "When the time is right. She grows clearer in my mind. I have seen her, and the wings, black as night, that she will carry at her back."

Evie closed her eyes and swallowed down a sob. When she looked up, the King was standing, reaching down to help her to her feet.

"Now we must hurry," he said, wrapping an arm around her waist.

"Where are you taking me?"

"To the Moon Pool. We must get you into its healing waters as quickly as possible. It has already been an hour since you drank from that cup."

"Why?" Something about the King's expression, and the fact that Evie suddenly realized that she could not have stood without his help, made her heart freeze. "What's wrong with me? What was in that cup?"

"Poison," the King said simply, and he pulled her from the room.

JAKE

The room he shared with Molly had never felt so small. Jake paced from one side to the other, like a lion caged too long, every nerve vibrating with tension, waiting for the sound of the knob turning, or the soft padding of Molly's feet in the hall.

The night had spun out of control in ways he never could have imagined. He had known for a long, long time that his life was a ship that was going down, fast and hard. He had only wanted to be with her, to steal a little of the sunshine that seemed to cling to the surface of her skin for himself before his time ran out. But now, for the first time, Jake realized he might carry Molly with him, down to the bottom of the sea. It scared him in ways that he didn't know how to process, made him angry and terrified in ways that he couldn't begin to understand. She had seemed so strong. So full of life and goodness.

It had never occurred to him that he could hurt her.

Now, he wished that he had died before he met her. He wished that the first time he had shot up, what felt like a hundred years ago, that his insides had twisted and seized, and he had died with that first, high-induced grin plastered eternally on his face.

The knob turned. Molly walked in, and Jake turned to face her, despair still raging in his heart. They stared at each other for a second, and Jake felt like there was no air in the room. Guilt and self-loathing surged like a tidal wave inside him, and for a moment he felt like he would never breathe again.

Then Molly smiled.

The expression seemed so sincere, so out of place, that Jake felt the impact of it like a physical blow to his body.

"What?" he asked, completely non-pulssed. "What is it?"

"It's going to be okay, Jake." Molly closed the door behind her, and walked over to him, her steps light and graceful. She sighed with relief, her eyes fluttering almost closed as the air rushed out of her. She ran a hand down his shoulder. "I talked to Andrew. We can still fix this. You're going to be okay."

"I . . . I don't understand," Jake stammered. "What are you talking about?"

"Andrew explained everything to me. Why I wasn't able to help you as much as you need. All we need is that goblet he's been so obsessed about. Andrew says once we have it, my voice will be strong enough to make you better." She stood on her tiptoes, so they were exactly eye to eye. He could see the determination shining there. She looked so happy. Almost serene.

It scared him.

"I'm sorry I didn't realize the truth sooner," she went on. "I guess I just didn't want to admit that you were still suffering. But now that I know, I can do something about this." She nodded to herself, the smile fading as her expression hardened. "I can fix this."

Cold understanding leaked through Jake's veins. For the first time ever, he stepped away from Molly, pulling back from her touch.

"What does Andrew want you to do?" he asked, not caring that his voice sounded hard and angry. He should have known. He should have realized a long, long time ago, the game Andrew was playing. Jake had seen it a hundred times before. But Andrew was hard to read. Magic and power swirled around him, layers of distraction and deceit. But now, finally, the truth was coming to the surface.

Molly's eyes clouded. She probably hadn't expected Jake to step away from her, didn't understand the coldness in his voice.

"He just needs me to help him get the goblet," she answered, defensiveness tinting her words. "My voice can affect whole groups of people at once, and he thinks there's a large group of guards protecting the goblet."

Jake stood, silent. Thinking through what she had said.

"So," he said, after a long moment, "Andrew wants you to risk your life getting this thing for him."

"It isn't just for him. Having it will make all the Echoes safer. And it means I'll be able to help you. Really help you." Molly's hands fell to her sides. "What is it, Jake? What's wrong?"

Jake ran his hands over his face. Anger coursed through him, and even though he wasn't angry at Molly, he knew it was leaking through his eyes, hardening the edges of his voice. But he couldn't stop it.

"It's the same old shit," he spit. "Andrew is just like any other dealer. They reel you in, nice and slow. They make out that they're your friend. And then, once they find the right angle, they gut you. Take everything you've got and more. Leave you twitching on the sidewalk behind them once they've gotten what they want."

Molly's expression morphed into one of concern. "I don't understand what you're talking about, Jake." She said, "Are you feeling alright? We've both had a really long, hard night. Maybe we should rest for a while. We can talk about this more in the morning."

"When?" Jake demanded, "When does he want you to do this?"

"He isn't sure exactly," Molly shrugged. "But soon."

"You have to tell him no," Jake said, his voice rough. "And if you think he won't take no for an answer, then you've got to run."

"I'm not going to tell him no," she said, her eyebrows climbing, "I want to do this Jake. I want to be able to help you for real."

"Don't you understand what he's doing?" Jake cried. "Andrew doesn't care about you, and he sure as hell doesn't give a damn about me. I've always thought there was something off about that guy. He looks like a predator when he's looking at you. There have always been things about him that just don't add up. What's the deal with Denise, that woman who's like me, but never leaves his apartment? What happened to Tyler? He betrayed Andrew, and I haven't seen him since. And now this." Jake's shoulders fell. His voice softened. "Can't you see that he's using you?" he asked, his voice almost pleading. "He has something he wants and he needs you to get it. It's as simple as that."

Molly's eyes had hardened as Jake spoke. "Maybe I'm the one using him." She said, "I'm not stupid Jake. I don't think that Andrew's some kind of saint. But I know what I care about." She straightened up taller, throwing her shoulders back. "I know what I'm willing to risk."

"You're saying that you're willing to risk your life for me?" Jake gave a scornful laugh, "How is that anything but stupid? You can't do this, Molly!" Jake knew he was yelling, but he couldn't stop himself. He ran his hands over the stubble on his scalp, looking around the room desperately as though searching for a way to make her listen. "You're playing right into Andrew's hands. I'm not worth it."

"To me, you are," Molly said quietly, dropping her eyes and looking at the floor. "To me, you're worth everything."

"Fuck," Jake whispered bitterly, to himself. "How the hell did we get here? How did I let it get this bad?"

He shook his head and stepped closer, grabbing Molly's arm, pulling her a step toward him, and staring into her eyes. "Please. Molly," he whispered. "Don't do this. Don't put yourself in danger for me. I'm begging you to stop. Keep yourself safe. Whatever path I'm on, whatever damage I've done to myself that can't be undone

. . . it's my fault. It is because of decisions I've made, mistakes that are mine, and mine alone. I don't want you to pay the price for those mistakes. I want you to live, to be happy . . . even if that's a happiness we can't share." He swallowed hard. "I love you, Molly. Please—don't let me ruin your life."

Tears were leaking from the corner of Molly's eyes, and she leaned into him so that their foreheads were touching. Jake closed his eyes and breathed in the scent of her. His whole body was shaking.

"I love you, too," Molly whispered, and the words were like a dagger to Jake's heart. "But I know that I can do this. I'm stronger than you think."

"No . . ." Jake started to say, but Molly leaned away from him, and something in her expression silenced him. She reached up to her shoulder, to the thick bracelet that she always wore, pulling it off slowly. He recognized the emotion that filled her eyes. Fear. Uncertainty.

"You've never asked me about my tattoo," her voice shook a little as the bracelet slid from her fingers and fell to the floor. She reached out and took his hand in hers, lifting his fingers and spreading them across the skin on her shoulder.

Confused, Jake gazed at the ornate skeleton key tattoo that covered Molly's shoulder.

He felt deep ridges in her skin. Long lines of puckered flesh.

"What . . ." Jake murmured, confused.

Wordlessly, Molly guided his fingers up and down her shoulder. For the first time, Jake saw the disfiguring scars that even the expert tattoo couldn't quite mask.

He looked up at her, not quite able to ask.

"He liked to hurt me," Molly whispered. She shrugged, as though disarming the tremble in her voice and the marks on her arm. "It was a long time ago."

Jake shook his head, his fingers gently stroking the wounds that would never fully heal.

"I didn't know," he said softly.

Molly pursed her lips. "I don't talk about it. There really isn't anything to say. When I was going through that . . . during that period in my life . . . I wasn't sure I could survive it. And even after I did, I was sure that I was so torn up, inside and out, that I couldn't ever be happy again." Molly took a deep breath. "I was wrong. I healed. And I found that I could be a version of myself that I had never dreamed of before. All those terrible things in my past . . . they were like a key to a door that had to open. In the end, they made me stronger than I had been before. They made me who I am." She lay a soft hand against Jake's flushed cheek. "I can do this, Jake. I am going to save you. I love you . . . I think I've loved you since the first time you came to watch me sing. You're worth the risk, Jake. To me . . . you're worth everything."

She leaned in and kissed him, and Jake kissed back helplessly.

In his heart, he knew there was nothing more he could say.

MOLLY

Eventually, Jake slept. Molly lay awake, watching him, her fingers linked with his, relishing the warmth of his body.

And she thought.

Jake had been sure that he hadn't gotten through to her. She had seen the despair in his eyes. Even now, while he slept, she could still see the tension on his face.

But she had heard every word he'd said. And now, with the room quite dark, she forced herself to think things through.

How much did she really know about Andrew? Matt and Thia and the rest of the Echoes all worshiped the ground he walked on. Molly had been suspicious of him at first but, gradually, he had won her over. Many of the others had told her that Andrew had saved their lives, creating the Refuge, and bringing them to safety before the Legacies could hunt them down. But, now that she examined her memories more closely, she remembered hesitation in Evie's voice when Andrew's name came up.

It might be true that Andrew was using her. Molly wasn't sure that bothered her much—as long as she could still get access to the power that could cure Jake. But what if Andrew was lying? Almost everything she knew about this goblet were things that

Andrew had told her. What if the goblet could only strengthen one person, and he used it for himself? What if it had some other power completely, and Andrew had just told her what he thought she'd want to hear? She was willing to risk her life for Jake. But she wasn't willing to take that risk on Andrew's word alone.

She had to be sure.

Moving carefully, so that she wouldn't wake him, Molly untangled herself from Jake's embrace. He moaned softly in his sleep as she left him, but rolled over onto his side without opening his eyes. Molly leaned over and picked her bracelet up from the floor, carefully pulling it back onto her arm. Then she cracked the door open and slipped out into the hall.

Swiftly, she headed straight for Andrew's rooms. She would have to confront him. Demand that he show her proof that what he had told her was true.

When she heard his voice coming toward her, it was pure instinct to step into a darkened corner. Andrew's voice boomed as he and several other Echoes swept down the hall. They walked right past her, and Molly held her breath until they were out of sight.

After only a moment's hesitation, she resumed her course, moving faster, and glancing over her shoulder as she went. Searching Andrew's rooms was riskier. She wasn't sure what would happen if she was discovered. But it was also a much better way to find out the truth.

She just had to hurry.

The door to his rooms was unlocked, and Molly slipped inside, grateful that the hall was empty.

Once inside, she stood uncertainly for a moment. The room looked exactly as it had the last time she had been in it. The fire still burned in the corner, filling the room with a flickering, orange glow. Maps and papers were strewn everywhere. The walls were covered in sketches of the goblet, that seemed to haunt Andrew's dreams, as well as his every waking moment.

Molly saw a thick leather journal laying on Andrew's desktop. She rushed over to it. The pages were worn with use, page after page filled with thick, scribbled notes. She leaned close to it, flipping through the pages feverishly, her heart beating fast.

The notes were clearly intended just for his own use because much of it was little more than gibberish to her. Sentence fragments and words that seemed insignificant underlined repeatedly followed by thick exclamation points drawn with a heavy hand. Most of it, she realized after a moment, had been written some time ago, when Andrew was still searching for the cup. She turned the pages rapidly, pausing as she got closer to the back.

"The goblet is the key to everything," Andrew had written, and Molly's breath caught in her throat. "It will remove the limits of our power, strengthening our voices beyond what we can even imagine now. It will make us as powerful as the Sirens, draining them of power and bestowing it on us. Weakening the Sirens so severely that they cannot even hope to take revenge on us once their power has become our own. The Life-Blood Goblet is our future. And it is nearly in our hands."

Molly drew in a long shaky breath. It was true then. The goblet would do what Andrew had promised. It would give her a way to save Jake.

On the opposite page, Andrew had drawn yet another sketch of the goblet and, in dark, thick letters above it, he had scrawled the words, "For Denise." That was curious. Denise was fully human, like Jake. Could it be Andrew hoped that if he had the goblet, some of its power could be given even to those who had no Siren blood at all?

A sound interrupted her, and Molly froze, hardly daring to move. The sound came from the doors leading to the rest of Andrew's chambers, where she had never been. The hairs on the back of her neck stood up as the sound came again; a high-pitched, mewling sound, like the whine of a wounded animal.

In the perfect silence of Andrew's study, with nothing but the faint crackle of the fire and the sound of her own heart beating in her chest, Molly waited, dread building in her heart. There was something so very *wrong* about that sound.

It came again, and before she could even think through what her decision meant, or what the consequences might be, Molly strode forward. Seizing the doorknob, she threw open the door and stepped into a narrow, darkened hallway lined with closed doors.

It wasn't hard to tell where the sound was coming from. Molly felt the pull toward the last door in the hallway, the need to know so strong she felt that she practically drifted over the floor, pulled the door open, and stepped inside.

The room was dimly lit, and in the moment it took her eyes to adjust, the smell hit her first: sweat, filth, and stale air.

Then she saw him.

The bars had been embedded deep in the concrete. They threw dark, thick shadows onto Tyler's huddled, naked form.

Disbelief was like a cool hand on Molly's forehead, and she stood, her mind refusing to process what she saw.

The last time she had seen Tyler had been on the night that he betrayed Andrew and the rest of the Echoes to Steele. That night, he had taken Jake and nearly beat him to death. She had attacked Tyler then, almost killing him herself. But she never, in a million years, would have wished on her worst enemy what had been done to this man.

His body was covered with bruises and dried blood. His eyes were wide, as he pressed himself against the far wall of his cell, staring at Molly with mindless terror.

"T … Tyler?" she asked, her voice shaking. She could hardly believe it was him. Tyler stared at her hard for a moment, then opened his mouth, as though to respond.

A sudden wave of shock made Molly's vision swim, and she reached out a hand to steady herself against the wall.

Andrew had cut out his tongue.

"Holy shit," Molly cursed quietly. She realized her hand against the wall was touching something metal. She looked over.

The key to Tyler's cage hung on the wall, right in front of him. Positioned so that the tortured man could always see it, but never reach it to free himself.

Molly's fingers closed around the key, and after a moment of fumbling, she had found the lock on the cell door. She turned the key and wrenched the door open.

"Come on," she told Tyler. "I hate you for what you did for Jake. But I can't leave you like this."

But Tyler didn't dive toward the opening, or scramble for freedom. He shook his head frantically, pressing himself harder against the cement wall, holding out his hands as though shielding himself from a blow.

"Come on," Molly urged him. "We don't have much time. I've got to figure out how to get you out of here."

"He won't go," Denise's toneless voice said from just behind her, and Molly gasped and spun around.

Denise stepped closer, standing just in the doorway to the room, her lips pressed together as she looked over at Tyler. "Andrew has broken him too completely for that. And besides, Andrew would never forgive you for depriving him of his second-favorite toy." She stepped forward and gently closed the door of the cell, making sure that it clicked into place. She slipped the key from Molly's numb fingers and hung it carefully back on its hook. Her black hair swung around her shoulders as she leaned in closer to Molly, whispering fiercely, "You can't do anything for Tyler. But you can still save yourself, and Jake. Get out of here. Quickly."

Molly nodded, her mind still reeling. "You're right," she whispered, "I'll go."

Just then, there was a loud click, as the door to Andrew's study opened. A second later, they could hear Andrew's voice booming, and the faint sound of another voice answering.

Denise's shoulder hunched, and she grabbed Molly's hand.

"Come with me!" she hissed, "There's a back way out. We have to hurry."

Molly followed without question, and Denise led her out into the narrow hallway and around the corner. Glancing over her shoulder to be sure that Andrew wasn't in sight, Denise pushed on a panel of wall, which slid back, revealing a long, dark tunnel.

"This is Andrew's secret escape route," she whispered to Molly, "It will take you all the way up to the surface. To the metro section. Go," she pushed Molly's shoulder, urging her into the opening. "You won't get lost. Just keep going, till the dark gets lighter."

"Wait," Molly whispered, as Denise began to shove the panel of wall closed again. "Can you get a message to Jake?"

Denise paused, her eyes narrow. Then she gave a sharp, bare nod.

"Just tell him I'll be back soon, and that he should lay real low. Until I come for him."

"Fine," Denise snapped. "Now go. Before you're the death of us all!"

The panel slid shut. Molly didn't wait for her eyes to adjust to the pitch black all around her. As quietly as she could, she scrambled down the dark passageway, her legs burning, and her whole body shaking with fear.

EVIE

"You gave me poison?" Evie cried. "Why?"

The King steadied her with his hands, even as he pulled her toward the door. "Every soul experiences great clarity in the moments before death." He explained. "It is just a small jump from there to prophecy. Your transformation will be easier now that your body is weakened. It will save you from the poison's effects . . . if you can survive it."

"And what if I had not passed your test?" Evie demanded. She blinked rapidly, refusing to acknowledge the way her vision was swimming.

The King stopped short. He straightened up and looked her directly in the eyes. "Then we would have done whatever we could to save you. *If* you had wished it." He paused. "If you had asked us not to save you, I would have respected your wishes, and let the poison take its course."

Understanding flooded her. If she had not been deemed worthy to become one of them, they would have allowed her to choose death over slavery. If she had wished.

They were in the hallway now, and forms crowded around them. Evie would have looked at them with fascination and fear, had not the pain that had been biding its time inside her chosen that moment to force itself to the surface. Her back stiffened, and she thrashed like someone having a seizure

The King's voice boomed, somewhere outside the pain. "Prepare everything, and quickly. It is time!"

Evie felt her eyes rolling back into her head, felt the darkness coming. She did not even have time to wonder if she welcomed it.

When she woke up, the night air was cold against her skin. She opened her eyes. They were outside. She couldn't even guess how far they had carried her, or where they were now. Palm leaves rustled overhead, and water whispered. She was lying on smooth, perfect stone, beside a small pool. Even through the pain that racked her body, Evie could not help but appreciate how lovely the pool was. The shape of a perfect teardrop, the edges of the pool were lined with white stones that glittered like jewels in the bright moonlight. The water was so clear that Evie could see, despite its depth, all the way to the bottom . . . every inch lined with mother-of-pearl stones glinting with a thousand colors. The surface of the pool gleamed, filled to bursting with reflected moonlight.

Looking at it, deep longing pulsed through her whole body. Evie scrambled to her feet and took a hurried, unsteady step toward the pool's shining water.

A hand clamped down on her shoulder, arresting her movement.

"Not yet, Evie," the King's voice whispered. "You are almost ready."

It was only then Evie realized a large group had gathered around. For a moment, she thought that she glimpsed Roman's face, anxious, in the crowd.

Several of the Watchers, females in white tunics, were tending to her, their jewel-colored wings stretched out behind them. One was pulling back her hair, another adjusted the dress they must have changed her into while she slept. Pale white to the point of translucence, it draped over her front and flared into a flowing skirt. Her back was left bare. It might have bothered her . . . she might have wondered who exactly had looked on while her clothes were being pulled from her body, if the pain hadn't bubbled up in her again, clawing now inside her throat.

A woman was holding a cup to her lips.

"What?" Evie shuddered. "More poison?"

"No." It was the King who answered. "The poison weakens your body. Makes it more susceptible to change. The pool gives you strength and healing. But this drink is what makes the change come."

Evie took it and drained it. She did not taste it, did not know if it was bitter or sweet.

She felt a sudden, burning pain against her back. And then another, as one of the women brought a knife down, slicing lengthwise, first one side of her back, and then the other. Her insides spasmed. Evie screamed and knew that she was dying.

Then her body was plummeting through the air. The King must have lifted her, but she didn't feel anything until the water hit her.

Until the pool reached out, like a living thing, and welcomed her home.

Evie sank down, deeper and deeper, until she was resting, motionless, against the bottom of the pool.

It didn't occur to her to breathe. She didn't feel the slightest need to. She just felt the water around her, felt it splashing against the sides of the pool, slapping over the edges. She felt it with some part of her consciousness that was outside her body, for she neither breathed nor moved, but lay with lips parted, eyes open and unmoving. The moon shone down on the little pool, its light so bright that at the bottom, against the white stones, it seemed as bright as morning. Brighter. The light was increasing, the light that poured down from the moon pulsating as it grew in intensity. But it was not like light from the sun. This light did not burn . . . it purified as it shone . . . it cooled. The moonbeams laid against the water and chilled it. The water pulled tight against itself. It stiffened. Something like thick ice formed, crusting over the top. Down, inside the pool, Evie felt the water thicken around her till it was not water at all. She floated in it, her arms wrapped around her legs, her eyes finally closing. For the first time in a long time, Evie felt completely at peace.

There was a voice with her, there in the water. Of course there was. Evie did not feel any surprise when the water around her began to whisper, and she knew without thinking that the words she heard were the Moon's own voice. It spoke to her not as a god, but as a parent. A parent so much gentler than any Evie had ever known before.

The moon whispered to her, as a mother sings to the child in her womb. And though Evie did not know the words, still . . . she understood completely.

A bright light shone for her and, calmly, she held it in her palm. With its light, she gazed from one end of her life to the other. In those moments, she knew with perfect clarity and accepted with complete serenity, everything that had happened to her, and all that was yet to be. She saw her life as a perfect whole, a song that you know all the way to the end, even though it is only half sung. She felt the very sound of her life vibrating in the water, and she smiled as it sang.

The change came slowly, awareness creeping back bit by bit so that she could not have said when it began. But, suddenly, she was aware that her back itched.

The itch grew.

It burned.

The burn grew till she kicked and flung out her arms, thrashing in the thick liquid. As she kicked, she rose, closer and closer to the surface.

Suddenly, she found that her face was pressed against a thick layer of ice. She did not like it. Fury, hot and red and unlike anything she had felt before, pulsed inside her.

Evie kicked the ice, pounded it. Again and again, her fist crashed against it, making no mark. The nails of her right hand stretched and lengthened, till they were not nails anymore, but the fierce, cutting claws of a predator. Thick, sliding out the pads of her fingers like cat's claws, her claws hit the ice and pierced it.

The ice cracked with a sound like thunder, shattering the silence of the night. Evie thrust her head out of the water, gasping and sputtering. Air felt foreign in her lungs. At the back, her thick wings trembled and flapped uselessly, dripping with water, struggling to unfurl. Hands were thrust at her from every direction, reaching to pull her out.

She pushed them away. They did not know her strength, did not know all the secrets the Moon had told her. Already, like a dream, all that she had known was fading away. Evie clung to the side of the pool. Gasping, she pushed her hair out of eyes and stared upward. The Moon smiled down at her.

Evie smiled back. Then she spread out her wings of leather, as black as night. And Evie soared.

MOLLY

It wasn't hard, once she decided what to do. And the understanding came quickly, almost effortlessly, as Molly made her way through the dark and then, cautiously, stepped through the hidden doorway and out into the metro station.

It felt strange to walk among humans, knowing that she wasn't really one of them. But there was no time to think about that now. Molly lowered her head and shoved her hands deep into her pockets, throwing herself into the crowd. Letting it swallow her up.

She went to the library first, where she worked quickly, and with intense focus. It helped knowing that money wouldn't be an issue. An hour on the computer and she had a list of phone numbers. She wanted the best there was.

She knew she'd have no trouble getting it.

Only when she stepped outside and felt the cold burning the back of her neck did it occur to her that she would need a car. That, too, took only a very few minutes. She refused to think about it. She walked into the dealership, smiled brightly at the first salesman she saw, and leaned in nice and close so that only he could hear her voice. Twenty minutes later, she was just outside the DC border, driving her new car well above the speed limit.

The world outside her window turned green with surprising speed. Soon there were golf courses on one side and sprawling, stone-built schools on the other. She glanced at the GPS frequently, careful not to miss the last turn. Then she was pulling into the long, twisting drive of Hope Pavilion.

The main thing, Molly thought to herself as she walked past the carefully manicured flower beds, was not to make a scene. To arrange everything quietly. The double doors in the front opened into a bright, welcoming area. Thickly cushioned couches covered with warm, bright colors sat beside deep bay windows. Even with all the obvious wealth around her, Molly did not feel the slightest bit out of place in her leather jacket and torn jeans. The woman at the half-circle front desk smiled warmly as Molly walked up.

"Welcome!" the woman said. "Can I answer any questions for you about Hope?"

Molly folded her arms on the desktop and leaned in close, talking softly, careful to keep a smile on her face the whole time. The woman never even flinched. She probably didn't even realize what Molly was doing. She smiled as her fingers moved on the keyboard, happy to help and arrange for anything that Molly asked. Soon, she was escorting Molly cheerfully to the director's office. There, too, Molly was cautious. She closed the door tightly behind her and scooted her chair next to the huge oak desk. Ten minutes later, she was strolling back to her new car. Everything was in place. The trip back to the city took less time than the drive out of it. She didn't have to check the map; here she was at home.

When she walked back into their room, Jake was sitting cross-legged against the wall, his eyes round and anxious. He jumped to his feet when he saw her, lurching toward her.

"Where have you been?" he gasped, taking her hands in his

own. He was sweating. "Denise gave me this strange message and told me that you left. I've been so worried."

"I'm sorry, Jake. Just come with me now, okay?" she tugged him toward the door. "I can explain everything. But I need you to come with me." Jake followed willingly, despite his obvious confusion, and followed her through the hallways. When they passed other Echoes, Jake hung his head and avoided their eyes.

No one stopped them as they walked toward the elevator. Still, Molly's pace quickened and Jake, picking up on her nervousness, matched her stride.

Soon they were outside. And though Molly had promised to explain everything, Jake asked no questions. He just slid into the car. Molly felt tired and tongue-tied. There was too much to say, and no way to say it. It was enough to be together. She reached out, and Jake took her hand in his. They held onto each other silently as the city faded in the rearview mirror.

It was only when they pulled into Hope Pavilion and the car came to a stop that Jake finally spoke.

"Molly?" he asked quietly, "What are we doing?"

Molly took a deep breath. "Jake, I need you to do something for me."

"I'd do anything for you."

"I know," Molly whispered. She closed her eyes for a second, bracing herself. Then she pushed open the car door. "So come with me. Please?"

They stayed close together, their shoulders brushing, as they walked slowly up the pavement.

"Good morning!" the woman behind the desk greeted them. "Welcome to Hope! You must be Jake."

Jake looked back at the woman blankly.

"Yes, that's right." Molly hurried to answer for him.

"I'll just tell Rebecca you're here."

She disappeared down the hallway. Jake looked down at Molly, his eyes widening in profound confusion.

"Molly?" he breathed. "What . . ."

She pulled him over to one of the thickly cushioned couches. There were small groups of people clustered together throughout the large room, families clutching coffee cups, teenagers dragging desperately on cigarettes. Couples sitting silently, hunched over tightly clasped hands. Molly looked at them sorrowfully. *Is this what hope looks like?* she wondered to herself.

To her, it looked an awful lot like despair.

"This is one of the best places in the country," she said, rushing her words. "I've arranged it all. Their top therapist cleared her whole schedule for the day. So that she can spend it with you."

"I don't understand," Jake whispered, and Molly could hear the rising panic in his voice.

"You were right to be suspicious of Andrew," Molly said, wrapping her hands around his. "I'm still going with him, to try for the goblet. But if something goes wrong . . . or if I don't come back." Molly shuddered, pushing memories of Tyler's wild face away. "You'll be safe here. They can help you."

"They can't." There was absolute certainty in his voice. "This won't work. Forget Andrew. Forget everything. Just the two of us. Let's just get out of here, Molly."

"And how long would that last, Jake?" Molly asked sadly. "How long until I find you in another dark hallway, with a needle in your hand?"

A woman cleared her throat delicately, and they looked up. She was much younger than Molly had expected. Her brown hair was pulled back in a ponytail. She wore jeans and a white, button-down shirt.

"I'm Rebecca," she said, and she reached out and shook their hands warmly. "Molly, if you don't mind, I'd like to start by speaking with Jake privately. Then, if he agrees, I'll meet with you privately, too. Does that sound okay?"

Jake looked at Molly desperately, and she gazed steadily back at him.

"Please," she whispered. "I'm not telling you to do this . . . I'm asking you. For me."

Jake looked at her silently, his eyes clouded and his hands sweating in her grasp. Finally, he gave a single, sharp nod. He stood up and followed the woman wordlessly back to her office.

Waiting was torture. It wasn't just that time slowed down; Molly felt like her body turned to stone. Worry and hopelessness wrapped around her like iron weights, pulling her down, down, down, till she felt sure she would sink right through the cushions and deep into the floor, back to the dark, narrow hallways that had somehow become her true home, to the grimy vault that she had come to think of as her tomb.

Finally, Jake came back out, his hands shoved deep into his pockets, his head hanging down. His eyes were edged with red.

"Molly?" Rebecca called. "Why don't we sit down together for a few minutes?"

Molly looked back anxiously at Jake, but he avoided her gaze. She turned and hurried down the hall to where Rebecca was waiting.

The office was not small, but it felt full. Rebecca's desk was piled high with papers, and books left face down and open. There were a few chairs and a loveseat clustered around a small coffee table, where an ashtray overflowed. Rebecca perched on one of the chairs, and Molly sat on the loveseat. They were silent for a long moment while Rebecca looked at Molly and Molly looked out the window. Molly got the distinct impression that Rebecca was struggling to decide what to say.

"Molly," she said at last. "Can you tell me how Jake went through detox?"

The question took Molly completely by surprise. She cursed herself silently for not anticipating these questions and thinking up reasonable answers. She could, of course, use her voice on Rebecca if she wanted to. But she feared it would make Jake's treatment fail.

"Well," she said slowly, "he hurt his hand."

"Okay," Rebecca answered carefully, nodding, with her face impassive, "and while he was recovering, he wasn't able to get the drugs he wanted?"

"I guess," Molly answered uneasily.

"And how, exactly, did he hurt his hand?"

Molly pressed her lips together and didn't answer.

Rebecca let the silence hang uncomfortably for a moment. Then she leaned forward.

"Molly, has Jake seen a doctor about that injury?"

"Sort of. A medic bandaged him up."

"But he didn't go to the hospital? See a specialist about any long-term nerve or tissue damage?"

She smiled reassuringly at Molly's horrified expression.

"It's okay," she said quickly. "It isn't uncommon for patients to come here with injuries or other health problems that have gone untreated. One of the first things we'll do is get Jake to a doctor who can determine what kind of help he needs. It does seem to me that he has lost a lot of function in that hand. He can barely move those fingers. He will certainly need some reconstructive surgery, and after that physical therapy, to get back as much movement as he can."

Molly's vision blurred for a split second, as a wave of horror flooded her.

"But it isn't hurting him at all!" she protested, trying to push back the shame that threatened to overwhelm her.

Rebecca smiled softly as she took out a notebook and began to jot down notes. "Well, that may be part of the problem," she said, still looking down at her paper. "Pain can be an awful thing, but it is the way our bodies tell our brain something isn't right. When that doesn't happen, it is easy to ignore an injury that desperately needs attention. Jake may be experiencing some nerve damage, or even possibly some brain damage from his drug use, which may prevent him from being aware of the pain in his hand. The doctors will try to figure it out."

Molly put a hand over her eyes. It wasn't nerve damage that kept Jake's hand from hurting. It was her. Her voice. It had never occurred to her that he might need more medical attention. He hadn't said anything, and once his pain had gone away, it had been so easy to forget . . . to pretend that the burn had been nothing more than a minor injury.

"Since Jake recovered from hurting his hand, how has he kept from relapsing?" Rebecca continued. "After my conversation with him, I have to admit I'm surprised that he's lasted this long."

"I've been with him most of the time," Molly answered evasively.

"And you help him to resist the temptation to use?"

Molly nodded.

"So, what made you decide to come here? Did something happen?"

"I realized that he isn't better," Molly said bleakly. "I had thought . . . really thought . . . that once the drugs were out of his system, he'd be okay. Once we were together, you know? I thought that I could . . ." She stopped, biting her lip.

"You thought you could keep him from relapsing?"

Molly nodded. Rebecca sighed and put down her notebook. "The families who come in here go through so much," she said. "So many of them truly believe that love should make it all better, that if they loved hard enough, the addiction would just go away. They're desperate to 'fix it.' Convinced that they can somehow force the person they love to get better. But, at some point, they all have to accept the same thing." She lay a hand over Molly's. "You can't. You can't *make* Jake better. I can't make Jake better. We can offer him support, tools, love, and encouragement, but ultimately Jake's recovery is up to him." Rebecca straightened up, pulling her hand away and clearing her throat delicately.

"Molly," she said. "I don't know exactly what kind of hold it is that you have over Jake . . ."

Molly started to protest, but Rebecca held up her hand. "I'm not judging. And if you think you're the first person to sit in my office who has more than one secret they want to keep, you're wrong. I once had a mother who hired a bounty hunter to forcibly remove her son from a crack house. A wife who shot her husband in the kneecap, and then promised to shoot him in the other leg, too, if he didn't swear to go into treatment. Loving someone, watching them destroy themselves . . . it can make us do crazy things. But if this is going to work, you have to accept the fact that Jake is an addict. And he always will be. No matter what you do, you can't force him to stay clean. This is his battle. His choice."

Molly shook her head. She liked Rebecca, and she was impressed by how much she seemed to have guessed. But she still couldn't agree.

"You're talking as though the drugs are part of who Jake is. Like, if suddenly all the drugs in the world disappeared and he couldn't take them anymore, it wouldn't make it better. Like they're part of him," Molly protested. "They aren't."

"But his reliance on them is," Rebecca answered firmly. "Jake's been using addictive substances since he was fourteen years old. At this point, they are hard-wired into his system. Using is a fundamental part of how he deals with the world around him . . . the way he copes with stress, with sorrow, even with joy. But I don't want you to be too discouraged." She lay her hand on Molly's knee. "He may never stop wanting the drugs. But he CAN learn to stop needing them."

Molly shook her head. "That isn't good enough," she said sharply. "I want him better. Healed. I want him to not be an addict anymore."

Rebecca leaned forward, resting her elbows on her knees. "Molly," she said gently. "Jake will be an addict for the rest of his life. A recovering addict, a sober addict, yes. That's what we can hope for. What we're going to fight as hard as we can to achieve. But it won't change the fact that he is an addict."

"I can't accept that."

"Why not?" Rebecca countered. "Being an addict doesn't have to be such a horrible thing."

Molly looked at her, her eyes full of disbelief.

"How can you say that?"

Rebecca shrugged. "Because I am one. I've been an alcoholic since I was sixteen years old. When I was twenty-two, my mother dragged me, half-dead, into detox. But I don't feel *any* shame when I say that I'm an alcoholic. Because the second half of that sentence is, and I've been sober eight years. Do you have any idea how much strength that takes? Do you have any idea how many liquor stores I've walked past in those eight years, how many bars? And each and every time I've wanted to go in, to have a drink . . . and every time I've resisted. Every. Single. Time. Recovered addicts are some of the strongest people I know. The most determined, the most focused. Bodybuilders, Olympic athletes . . . they don't even begin to compare. It's why I love my job, the reason I keep doing it even though I don't get happy endings nearly as often as I'd like. Because the ones who can do it, the ones who can find the will to make life different for themselves . . . they're the most beautiful, most inspiring people I know. You have to believe in Jake, Molly. This is his chance to find his strength, to prove to himself that he can do it. He has to realize that he has that ability. If he does, it will change everything for him. Life is never the same again, once you find strength like that inside yourself."

Molly's fingers strayed to her forearm, tracing her tattoo. Is that what she'd been doing? With all her power, all her love, all her desire to protect him? Had she somehow robbed him of the chance to protect himself?

"I think I understand what you're saying," she said. "But if you could do something for someone that you loved . . . if you could take a burden from them . . . wouldn't you have to do that? Wouldn't you have to try?"

"You're already doing the right thing, Molly," Rebecca said softly. "You're giving him love, support. You've brought him here. So many addicts don't have anyone like you pulling for them, someone who accepts who they are and hopes for who they might grow to be. Your love can't fix it, can't just make everything the way you want it to be. But it helps. It helps very, very much."

"You say that," Molly said slowly, "but I've seen the statistics. I know the relapse rates. Most people never recover from addictions like Jake's. Even with the best care in the world, how often do your patients really stay clean for their whole lives?"

Rebecca stood up and smiled sadly. "Not as many as I'd like," she admitted. "That's why we call our facility 'Hope.' Because it's what we have for each and every one of our patients. No matter what the statistics say. Let's go talk to Jake," she said, motioning for Molly to follow. "If he'll agree, I'd like him to start treatment here today."

Jake was sitting, drinking coffee on one of the couches in the front, and Molly sat down next to him. They held hands. "Jake," Rebecca began, "I'd like you to sign yourself into one of our residential treatment programs. I don't want to put too precise of a time limit on it right now, but I'd like you to stay with us for at least thirty days. How does that sound to you?"

Jake was nodding as Rebecca spoke. Without even looking in Molly's direction, he replied, "I'll do it," with a speed that took Molly by surprise.

"Great." Rebecca smiled warmly. "Did you bring some things with you?"

"No," Jake started to answer, but Molly interrupted.

"Actually," she said, "I have a duffel bag of stuff for you in the trunk."

"Great," said Rebecca. "Will you come and sign the paperwork now, Jake?"

"Can we have a few minutes to say goodbye?"

"Of course. Take as much time as you like. I'll go check with our in-house physician, and see if he can see you about your hand today." She stood, and Jake and Molly stood too.

"I'll see you in a few minutes, then," she said brightly. "I'm excited for you, Jake."

"Thanks," he said, "for everything."

She reached over and squeezed his shoulder before walking away.

They pulled the bag out of the trunk and then walked to a bench nearby, sitting silently, watching the wind push the bare branches of the trees back and forth above them.

"Molly," Jake said, "I'll do this. I'll try as hard as I can. Now, please . . . tell me you won't go along with Andrew's plan."

Molly took a deep, shaky breath. "I'm still going," she said quietly.

Jake turned to her, his eyes wild.

"I love you, Jake," Molly said, the words rushing out. "And I'm going to take care of you in every way that I can. It's as simple as that. That's why I needed to bring you here. I needed to know that, if I don't come back, you'll at least have a chance."

"Molly . . . what are you saying?"

"I'm saying . . . stay, Jake. Stay here, and get better. Heal as much as you can. And take all the things that won't heal, and turn them into muscle. You know that, as long as I'm alive, I will always come to you, right? You know that."

Jake nodded.

"So if I don't come back . . . you'll know. I will love you for my whole life. Whether that means for the next few days, or for the next eighty years, it'll still be just as true."

She leaned in and kissed him. He kissed back desperately, pressing his hands to the back of her head, pulling him hard against her.

"I won't let you go," he stammered. "I can't."

"Goodbye, Jake," Molly said and pulled his hands away. She heard him call after her as she turned and ran to the car, but she didn't stop or look back. She didn't pause to wipe the tears away as she pulled the car out of the lot and tore away down the street, leaving hope behind.

BEA

It was a strange sort of fairy tale that she had fallen into, Bea sometimes thought, as the days passed. One shot through with sadness. But she would take it . . . she wanted every second she could get. Bea seized hold of the fantasy that had caught her by surprise and hung on tightly. She walked through her days gingerly, willing the magic not to break.

She refused to wonder about the mystery of the lighthouse that had so quickly become her home. When footsteps scuffled somewhere far below, Bea did not look up. When a pot clanged late in the night, Bea rolled over and went resolutely back to sleep. She wanted to keep dreaming.

It was harder to pretend that her body wasn't changing. She and her angel both knew that she was getting worse; both had eyes open enough to see how quickly her strength was diminishing, how desperately tired she now was, all the time. Days passed, and the moon edged closer to fullness. Bea and her angel wrapped their heartbreak in silence, and loved each other with a fierceness that bordered on despair. And for a brief, precious time, they lived in a world that was entirely their own.

Until one day.

That day her angel woke up early. Bea had been sleeping, but he roused her, something he had never done before. The sun was just rising. As soon as she looked in his eyes, all sleep fled from her.

"What?" Bea whispered, reaching up to catch his face in her hands. But her angel shook his head, taking her hand and pulling her with him to stand across from the red door. Watching it.

Bea stood motionless beside him, glancing worriedly between his face and the door. Her angel was avoiding her eyes, but the hand that gripped hers was clammy. He was trembling. There was a loud thudding noise downstairs, and a knock. A door creaked open, and then shut with a bang. Her angel turned to look at her—and his eyes were full of fear.

It felt wrong to see someone so powerful shaking and afraid. Bea was shocked, but the shock somehow steadied her. A rush of adrenaline swept through her veins, and the frantic beat of her heart slowed. Bea felt stronger. She squeezed his hand.

There were footsteps on the stairs.

In that moment, Bea understood several things quite clearly. She knew that she loved this creature, the one who had pulled her from the water, who saw beauty in her scars, who had filled this last chapter of her life with beauty. She loved him fiercely. And Bea knew the truth: her sickness had reached the fullness of its measure. The trajectory of her life, plotted by some hand other than her own, had run its course. And underneath that sickness, or even wrapped tightly around it, Bea knew herself. Knew her strength. Knew the toughness that she had shared so proudly with her grandfather, and felt it, like unvarnished steel, still sharp and steady deep inside her.

The tread of footsteps came closer, and Bea's angel let go of her hand. The door creaked on its hinges, and her angel slid to the floor, falling to his knees, pressing his face deep into the blood-red carpet.

"Shit!" Bea hissed, shocked to see him fall. Instinctively she moved forward, stepping in front of him. Shielding him. As the door swung open, Bea closed her eyes for half a second and took a deep, deep breath.

And Bea knew that her fairy tale was ending.

The figure that entered wore a tunic, not much different from the one Bea wore but made of deepest gold. His hair was shoulder-length and wavy brown. His great wings, coated in snow-white feathers, furled out behind him like great white sails riding the crest of the wind.

He looked at Bea as she stood, her legs braced shoulder-length apart, her eyes burning.

"Who the *fuck* are you?" Bea demanded, "What do you want from us?"

"I mean you no harm, Beatrice," the King said, holding up his hands, as though to show that he carried no weapon. "You are honored and welcomed among us. Neither do I mean any harm to your love." He looked over her shoulder, to where her angel still knelt, prostrate, on the rug. "Rise, Malachi," he commanded, and her angel stood.

It was the first time that Bea had ever heard his name.

"My name is Gideon. I am king of our kind, and I have come to speak with you. Malachi, you must leave us for a while."

"No." Bea reached behind her, and wrapped her thin hand around her angel's arm, stopping him mid-stride. He had already started to leave, obeying his king, but at Bea's touch, he froze, looking at her with surprise. "Whatever you have to say, you say to both of us."

The King raised one eyebrow, displeasure plain on his face.

Bea took a step toward him, and spoke in a whisper, "You think you can walk in here, scare the man I love half to death, and then start ordering us around?" Bea shook her head. "You may be his king, but you sure as hell aren't mine. Tell us what you want, and then get out." She crossed her arms over her chest. "I don't have time for this shit."

The King rocked back on his heels, his eyes taking her measure. Bea met his stare, daring him to test her.

"Very well," he said icily, the words forced and choppy on his lips. "He may stay. But that will not make what I have to say any easier to hear." He closed the red door behind him and strode to the center of the room, standing with his back to the windows. For a second, Bea's eyes wandered over his shoulder, to the beckoning blue of the ocean. She thought of white sand beaches, of water skimming under her fingers as her angel carried her through the air.

"I have long needed to speak with you. To ask you to help us," the King said, and Bea's eyes snapped back into focus. "Perhaps I have waited too long."

His gaze ran over her, and Bea saw her illness reflected in his eyes. She saw pity swell there, and hated him for it.

"Why would you need to speak with me?" Bea demanded. "You're some kind of sparkly-white supernatural creature. What can I possibly do for you that you can't do for yourself?"

"We have made an error. *I* have made a terrible error, and I fear that my people," he stretched a hand toward Bea's angel, "will pay the price. There is an object that can do us great harm. It pulls the life force out of us and bestows it on another. There are people who are seeking that object, planning to make themselves powerful. And to destroy us."

Bea glanced over at her angel. Ten minutes ago, it would have been hard for her to imagine that anything could be a threat to him. But she could see the fear in his eyes, could see from the expression on his face that this stranger spoke the truth.

"And what does that have to do with me?" Bea asked, her eyes narrowing.

"I wasn't sure, when I first glimpsed you in my dreams, why your fate was intertwined with my people. Still, I told Malachai where to find you the night that he pulled you from the waves."

Bea looked at her angel, who stood as though defeated, his

head bowed low against his chest. Her hand still rested on his arm, steadying him, ready to pull him back to his feet if he started to crumble again.

"Is that true?" she whispered, and he nodded, not looking up. Bea turned back toward the King.

"So, what are you saying? That you sent him to get me?"

"I did not send him. I only told him of you, and of what I had seen. I said that, if he went to you, he would find a love he could not keep. He did not intend to rescue you. He told me it would be cruel. He went, I think, only to be close. To see you. But, in the end, his heart did not give him a choice."

"Wait a minute." Bea was holding her free hand up in front of her, fending off his words. "He told you? What do you mean he told you?" There was a moment of silence. For the first time since he had entered, the King looked uncertain. Bea's voice was small. "He can speak?" She spun to look at her angel. "You can speak?"

Slowly, warily, her angel nodded.

"If you can speak, why won't you speak to me?"

It was the King who answered. "Surely, you have guessed the truth by now, Beatrice. You must know."

Bea shook her head numbly, her eyes still locked on the one she loved. "No," she whispered. "I didn't think about it. I didn't want to. I just . . ." Bea's voice grew softer, and a little hoarse. "I just took what life gave me, and didn't wonder about it. It was so much more than I had hoped to have. Such a miracle. It felt wrong to look at it too closely."

"And now?" the King asked.

Bea closed her eyes.

"Tell me," she said.

"Malachai can speak, child, but he does not dare to speak to you. He carries the curse of our kind. If you heard his voice, even for a moment, even a single word, your mind would be destroyed. Your will would no longer be your own. He could not keep the hurt from you, no matter how dearly he loved you."

Bea opened her eyes and looked her angel full in the face. He lifted his head slowly, pressing his lips together as he met her gaze, as though bracing himself for a blow that was sure to come.

"And the noises that I've heard downstairs?" Though she spoke to the King, Bea did not look away from Malachai.

"Those who serve him live below."

"Slaves?"

"Criminals," The King's voice hardened. "We have laws, and Malachai has always been faithful to them. The ones who serve him do so out of love, and only after their own vile acts had condemned them."

"He didn't want me to see," Bea whispered.

"Perhaps he did not want you to know."

Bea took a step closer to her angel. "You were afraid I would hate you, once I knew what you are." It was not a question.

He looked back at her steadily, not blinking, not letting any emotion show on his face. Bea lifted her hand, trailing her fingers slowly down his chin, and over his Adam's apple. Standing on tiptoe, she put her lips next to his ear.

"Every part of you is beautiful to me," she whispered, leaning in to kiss his neck. "Always."

A shudder ran through him as his arms jerked upward, pressing her to him. They clung to each other for a long moment, not caring that the King stood only a few feet away.

"Wait," said Bea, a moment later. She pulled away a little, still keeping her arms wrapped around her angel's waist. "If the curse of your kind is that you can't talk to humans, then how are we even having this conversation?"

"As king, I carry a different curse. I bear the curse of prophecy, instead."

"How is that a curse?"

"Because of what my dreams sometimes show me. And last night, I dreamed a wave of red. An endless, moonless night. Our entire people, drained of power and then hunted down until not a single one remains."

Bea's arms tightened around her angel. Somehow, she could no longer laugh at the King's dreams.

"But that is not all I saw," the King went on. "I dreamed of two keys, one made of silver, the other of red. The first opens the door. The second opens herself."

"What does that mean?"

"You are the second key," the King said, something unfathomable in his eyes.

A strange sensation washed over Bea, one that lifted her out of herself. The feeling that she had had this conversation before, that the words that were about to be spoken were known to her already, somewhere deep inside. She just couldn't quite remember.

"Speak English!" she growled at the King, but there was no real bite in her words. "What are you trying to tell me?"

"You can stop the bloodshed. You can protect the one you love, and keep a terrible power from falling into the hands of those who would misuse it." But the words he spoke did not match the somber expression on his face.

"The rest . . ." Bea demanded. "Tell me the rest."

The King hesitated. "There would be a price," he said. "A heavy one. You can save his life only at the cost of your own."

Bea closed her eyes and exhaled a long, slow breath she hadn't known she was holding. The King kept talking, his words anxious now, and hurried. "There is a goblet. It pulls the life-blood from us and gives our power to another. There is only one way to destroy it: it must be used by a human, whose body could never absorb the power that it holds. Used by a human, the power that it holds would flow through you, and then, finding nothing to latch onto—would flow back into the goblet itself. Overwhelming it, and destroying it forever." He paused, as though waiting for Bea to say something, but she did not move, did not open her eyes. "But it would kill you, child," the King said softly. "Slowly. And with pain."

Bea found herself nodding, her eyes still squeezed shut, lost in her own world of gray and gold. It made a sort of sense. Formed a twisted kind of symmetry.

"Okay," she murmured, forcing herself to pull air into her lungs, trying to steady her thoughts. "Okay."

Suddenly fingers were clutching her arm, her angel's hands clamping painfully against her skin, pulling her toward him. Bea's eyes snapped open, and her angel was shaking his head furiously, his eyes wild.

"You must know," the King continued, raising his voice, "that this request comes from me alone. I spoke to Malachai late last night. He did not want me to request your help. But he could not keep me from coming."

Bea tore her eyes away from her angel's silent pleas and turned toward the King. "I understand," she said. "I'll do it."

The sound that exploded behind her was worse than any she could have imagined, worse than steel screaming as two cars collided, worse than a wounded animal howling in the darkest part of the night. It was a moan, deep and guttural and full of anguish.

"**Malachai**!" the King shouted. Bea turned. Her angel's face was flushed with red, his eyes wild. His fingers pulled at his own hair. His chest swelled, while his face contorted with misery.

"Control yourself!" the King cried out. "You will destroy her!" He strode forward, hands outstretched; but Bea got there first.

"Listen to me!" she half-demanded, half-pleaded, taking her angel's flushed face between her hands, forcing him to look at her. "Listen! You can't save me. We've known that ever since the first day . . . ever since you pulled me from the water, we've known where this was heading. We can hide from it all we want, we can pretend that we can't see . . ." She took his hand in hers and pressed it against her chest. "But it's here." Her voice broke. "It is going to take me from you. I would have stayed with you, my love, forever. I would have made you my eternity. But it doesn't matter how hard I fight; it doesn't matter how strong or brave I am . . . I can't stop it." She half-smiled, tears running down her face. "I'm not used to being weak. I don't like it. But this . . . destroying that goblet. Protecting you. That is something I *can* do. I can keep you safe! Don't you see? See how much easier it is for me to die for a reason than it would be for me to slowly inch along, crumbling as I go? I can do something for you that no one else can do. Isn't there a kind of poetry in that? A kind of beauty? When you did something for me that no one else in the whole wide world could have done. You healed my heart when the rest of me was so very broken. You have to let me do this. Okay? Please. I need you to understand."

Her angel stared into her eyes, his hand clutching at hers. He closed his eyes and gave a small, sharp nod.

"I will come back for you at the end of the week," the King said, retreating toward the door, whether to give them privacy or to escape from the misery in the air, Bea was not sure.

"No," she said, and the King froze. She turned to look at him. "Come tomorrow," Bea ordered. "I'm not sure how much time I have."

The King half-bowed. "Very well," he agreed. "I will return at first light." Then he was gone, the red door clicking shut behind him.

As soon as they were alone, Malachai stumbled to the windows, throwing them open as though he were suffocating, sitting down hard on the edge. He sat bent over, his hands pressed over his mouth. Bea could see his shoulders convulsing, and knew he feared that the sounds of his sobs would rip her will away.

"Do you need me to leave?" she asked uncertainly, but he reached back, his hand grasping blindly until it found hers, pulling her to him. Bea sat with her arms wrapped around him, her face pressed against his arm. For a very long time, they sat, mourning together. When he finally looked up at her, Bea reached up and wiped the tears from his cheeks.

"I don't know where I'll go . . . after it happens," she whispered fiercely. "But I know . . . I *know* that my love will never leave you."

JAKE

That first day had passed in a blur. Jake remembered the intake doctor reaching out and saying, "Let's take a look at this hand," as he unwrapped the bandage. He had whistled through his teeth when he saw it. Jake thought that was unprofessional.

"When exactly did this happen?" the doctor asked, holding Jake's hand gingerly and pressing against it very lightly in one place and then another.

"Two months ago?" Jake had answered uncertainly. "No. Maybe just one month?"

"And you haven't seen a doctor, all this time?"

"Someone bandaged it up for me," Jake answered defensively.

"I can see that." The doctor's sarcasm wasn't even subtle.

"How bad is it?"

"Well, wiggle those fingers around for me as much as you can."

Jake knit his eyebrows together and did his best. The doctor whistled again.

"Pretty bad, I'd say. How much does it hurt you?"

"Not at all."

The doctor looked at him, long and hard. "Not at all, you say?"

"Nope."

The doctor took a roll of fresh bandages out of a drawer and began to wrap Jake's arm again.

"Well, this is far and away beyond what I can handle here. I'm going to write you out the names of three different specialists that I want you to see."

"Three?"

"That's just for starters. You've had a severe injury, and the fact that it's gone untreated so long will make dealing with it even harder." He tsked quietly under his breath.

"And as the drugs you've got going in your system wear off, the pain is going to be a big problem too. Painkillers are usually not allowed for patients in rehab, so you'll have to talk to your counselor about different options."

Jake nodded, not bothering to try to explain that he had no drugs in his system, and the pain would not come back, not as long as Molly was alive. Worry flared in his chest, burning him. He wished for a cigarette.

"Let's take a look at the rest of you," the doctor said mildly. He pulled the white gown away from Jake's skin. It hadn't even occurred to Jake to think of the marks that covered his back. The wounds from Tyler's beating had closed up, but deep injuries like that took a long time to heal. He felt the doctor freeze behind him.

"You've really been through hell, haven't you son?" he said at last.

"Yeah," Jake admitted. "More than once."

After that, Jake moved in a fog, a deep white fog that softened all the sounds around him, and made the edges of his vision blur. He put his duffel bag on the bed that they pointed out to him; he carried the schedule of sessions with him as he went from place to place. But his mind was always with Molly.

He knew she was alive. That, at least, he couldn't doubt. He felt the link between them, like skin pulled too tight over a wound, stretching and jerking at him somewhere deep in his chest. *Would*

I know if she was in pain? Would I know when the danger started? he wondered as he sat in the back of the group therapy sessions. He fell into bed that first night with nothing else on his mind.

She wants me to be here, Jake reminded himself as he lay, sleepless, in the dark. *This is what she asked me to do.*

He liked talking with Rebecca, and she spent a lot of time with him. And, oddly, he found he liked going to the family therapy sessions. He didn't have any family with him, but no one kicked him out. He couldn't even have said what drew him to it, but he found it fascinating. The couples held hands tightly, but they didn't look at each other. The parents who sat with their arms wrapped around the too-skinny teenager between them, faces pale with guilt and worry, fighting a last-ditch battle to save their child from a villain who had no face and lived beneath his very skin.

Here, more than anywhere else, Jake felt awake. He followed the conversations closely, watched the faces of the other patients with interest. It was like he was looking for something . . . searching for his sister in the faces around him. Jake felt lonely when he sat there, and jealous. Jealous of the other addicts, who at least had someone there to sit beside them. It hurt, but he sought the pain out. He held onto it like he wanted to look at it and understand exactly what it was. What would life have been like, Jake wondered, if on that day so long ago, instead of closing the door in his face, his sister had offered to drive him to detox? He felt sure that he would have gone. The truth was that Molly was the first . . . but, no. He would not think of Molly.

The day that everything changed, the session started out like all the others. People chatted together and then quieted down when the therapist began the session. Jake noticed a young couple that he vaguely remembered having seen around before. The girl looked young, like a cheerleader: painted nails, high heeled shoes, softly curling blond hair that fell down around her shoulders. The boy was gaunt, and seemed too young to be a husband and a father and an addict, all at once. Jake understood that their baby was only a few months old.

Halfway through the session, Jake's focus had begun to wander. He was looking out the window, picking at the bottom of his shoe. He didn't even know what it was that made the blond-haired girl stand up and start shouting. She rounded on her husband, leaning over him.

"But that's exactly what you're doing!" she screamed, her face just inches from his. "Don't you think you can talk like that! Don't talk about yourself . . . as though what you do doesn't affect us all. Don't you realize? You're a part of us . . . we're supposed to be a family! Everything you do to yourself . . . you're doing it to us, too! Every time you put that needle in your arm, you might as well be putting it into mine!" She held out her arm, smooth and perfect and un-scarred, up under his nose and waved it back and forth. "Or into Chrisse's arm. She's only a baby . . . only three months old. But she's already scarred. Already *ruined*! By you! By what you've done to us . . . to our family! You don't get to talk like that . . . not anymore . . . like you're deciding what kind of life you want for *you*! You're choosing for all of us—hurting all of us! You're hurting *me*. Jesus, Ken! You're hurting that beautiful baby we made together!" And she reached over, and slapped her husband, hard, across the face.

"Jesus," Jake muttered to himself.

The small room exploded with exclamations and cries.

"Okay, okay. Calm down, everybody. Why don't we take a break here for a minute?" The counselor was breaking it up, and everyone got up and moved to the door. Jake moved with them, walking out to the hallway. He stood in front of a window, looking out but seeing nothing.

"Jesus!" he said to himself again, rubbing his eyes.

For some reason, an image rose in his mind. Crystal clear, as though it was happening in front of him, he imagined the gaunt boy standing over a crib. The tiny, blonde-haired baby was fast asleep. She didn't see her father, or the needle he held in his hand until he was pressing it deep into her vein. The child woke, screaming . . .

"Oh, God," Jake muttered and started walking blindly. The image was too horrible, too solidly real in his mind. But as soon as that image faded, another took its place. He saw himself with Molly, in their little room. Molly was sleeping. And Jake imagined himself, his face dead and full of malice, leaning over her, holding her arm steady as he plunged a needle deep into her vein . . .

"Oh, my God," Jake said again. He was shaking; he felt like he might fall down. He stumbled out to the garden, where the sun was already setting. Everything was gray. He sat down heavily on a bench and held his head with his hands. His mind was racing.

He hadn't wanted to be alone. He had wanted Molly—her touch, her love, everything. He had fooled himself into thinking that he could take that love for free, just for a little while. That he could grab that little bit of comfort, and then go on along his needle-paved path of self-destruction. But he had been wrong . . . so very, very wrong. There would be a terrible price. But he wouldn't be the one to pay it.

Molly would.

Without him even realizing it, he and Molly had become a unit. Their own little family, of just two broken people who loved each other despite all the craziness in their world. And now that they were bound up like that, everything he did affected her. Every mistake he made came at a cost to them both.

Jake sat and sat, even after the sun had faded completely from the sky. After a long time, he realized that his ears and nose were burning from the cold. He looked up at the sky.

The full moon loomed above him.

Molly would have left by now. She would already be on her way to the cave.

Jake got up, stumbling, his feet numb from the cold, and threw himself down on his bed. He slept, but even as he drifted off, he was thinking. When he dreamed, his mind was awash in a new clarity, as though a light he had never known he possessed had flared to burning deep inside him.

He woke up in the morning, his thoughts from the night before still an unbroken chain.

"God," he said to himself, wonderingly. "I've got to go."

He pulled the duffel bag out from under his bed and slung it over his shoulder. He hurried out of the tiny room without a backward glance.

It wasn't hard to find Rebecca, cradling her first cup of coffee in her hands as she unlocked her office. "What's going on, Jake?" she asked, her eyes taking in the bag slung over his shoulder, disappointment already written on her face.

"I didn't want you to get the wrong impression," Jake said, standing in the doorway as she pushed open her door. "I wanted to let you know that I'll be back in a couple of days."

Rebecca shook her head as she bent over to switch on her desk lamp. "You can't just walk out of rehab, Jake. Here, come on in. I don't have any appointments until nine. Why don't you sit down and talk with me for a minute?"

Jake hesitated. He knew that he had to move quickly. But he had come to really respect Rebecca, and to trust her. He checked his watch as he walked in and sat down on the couch.

"Okay," he said. "But I can only stay for a minute."

Rebecca settled herself into an over-sized chair, tucking her feet up under her. "What's going on, Jake? You've been making so much progress, and I've felt like our sessions have been really productive. What would make you consider leaving?"

"I'm not giving up," Jake said firmly. "I believe in doing this. For the first time, I really feel like I can."

"That's wonderful, Jake!" Rebecca beamed at him, her smile quirking up. "But then why am I sitting here, trying to talk you into hanging around?"

"There's a situation," Jake said awkwardly. He had told Rebecca so much about his life, his childhood. It was hard to remember that some secrets weren't his to tell. "Something that I have to do. Once it's under control, I'll come right back."

Rebecca's eyebrows scrunched together, as they always did when she was trying to work through something he had said.

"Did you get a call, or a letter, from someone last night?"

"No," Jake admitted.

"So this situation, the one you don't want to tell me about . . . you've known about it for a while?"

"Yeah. I guess."

"So what's different, that yesterday you were going to sessions, and this morning you're walking out the door?"

Jake shifted uncomfortably in his seat. How did she always understand the things he didn't say out loud, as much as the things he did say?

"I went to a session last night. Family therapy."

Rebecca's eyebrows inched up slightly, but she made no comment.

"Something happened there. There was a woman, a girl, really. She's married to this user. She freaked out . . . started screaming at him . . ."

"I heard about it," Rebecca commented dryly.

"It was intense." Jake shook his head. "Afterwards, I went outside, and I sat for a long time. Just thinking. And I thought . . ." His voice faltered. Rebecca looked down at the floor, giving him space.

"There's no rush, Jake," she said, studying the carpet. "Take your time."

"My mom never gave a shit." Jake cleared his throat savagely. "There was never even a question. My sister . . . she cared when we were little, but once I was in deep, she cut and ran—didn't even need to stop and think about it. Didn't even hand me a twelve-step brochure, or offer to drive me to AA. Just showed me the door. I mean, I tried, a couple of times. Detox, I mean. I never made it to the other side."

"It's hard to do on your own."

"That's just it!" Jake leaned forward. "I've always been on my own. Always. In my mind, it was always about me versus the detox, me versus the rehab, me versus all this shit that seemed so painful and hard." He shrugged. "It was never worth it. I could never win out against that kind of math."

Rebecca's whole face was scrunched up now, her eyes narrowed with concentration. "Help me understand what you mean, Jake. What kind of math are we talking about?"

Jake exhaled with frustration, running his hand over the sharp bristles on his scalp. It was clear inside . . . why was it so hard to say it out loud, in a way that didn't sound insane? "The math I did in my head. I knew I was on my own. I knew I was killing myself, even, but I didn't give a fuck about that. Nobody did. But it's different now."

"Tell me how it's different."

Jake felt himself smiling, though he could just as easily cried. "It isn't just me anymore. That changes the math, changes everything. That's what the woman was trying to say last night. When someone else's life is tied up in yours, when your using hurts them even more than it hurts you . . . the equation is totally different."

Rebecca had lit a cigarette, and she tapped it thoughtfully against the ashtray. "You're saying that you can do for Molly something that you couldn't do for yourself. That you can get sober for her sake."

"Not exactly," Jake said. "It's also that it changes me. I mean, when someone throws in with you like that, when they say that they're with you, that if your ship goes down, they're going down with it . . . it changes everything. I couldn't do it before . . . I really couldn't. I was so empty inside; I needed something, anything, that would fill me up. But now . . ."

Jake stood, slinging his bag back over his shoulder.

“I'm not so empty. I can fight. For the first time I feel like I could do this, could stay clean. And I can do more than that. I can stand up for myself against the drugs. *And* I can fight for the person who's supposed to be with me in those family sessions.”

“I respect what you're saying, Jake, I really do.” Rebecca set down her coffee cup and spread her hands out on her knees. “But I want you to stop and think about what walking out of rehab means. I know you think you can just go out for a bit, and then come back and pick up right where you left off. But the reality is that once a patient walks out, they hardly ever make it back. If you walk out now, before you've really gotten to the other side, it's a terrible risk. I don't think Molly would want you to take that chance. Whatever challenges she might be facing, I *know* that she would want you to stay.”

“That's part of it, too.” Jake smiled. “I love Molly, but that girl last night showed me something else, too. The biggest battles we fight are inside ourselves. We can’t fight those battles for the people that we love. But sometimes, you can help to keep them on course. And when you love someone . . . really love them . . . sometimes you have to slap 'em in the face. Molly’s making a terrible mistake. And I have to stop her.”

“The door is always open, Jake!” Rebecca's voice called after him as he hurried down the hall. “I'll be waiting for you to waltz back in here and prove me wrong!”

Molly had left some money in the bottom of the duffel bag she gave him. It would have to be enough. Jake caught a cab and sat slumped in the back seat, going over his plan again and again in his mind. After the initial thrill of deciding, of rushing out into the world full of purpose, now doubt was pulsing through him. His plan was full of holes. He knew it, and it wasn't hard to think of dozens of things that could go horribly wrong. But still, he smiled to himself as he passed the cash into the front seat and slid out of the cab, melting immediately into the crowd milling through the station.

He was going to do it anyway.

He rounded the corner and casually walked on, past all the other people, to the shadowy corner at the end of the platform. His stomach clenched when he saw the elevator.

This is crazy! a voice in his head warned him. *Any one of these people could tear you to pieces, and you wouldn't even be able to say a word!*

He had a key. He had palmed one, long ago, inspired by an addict's instinct to collect useful objects. He ground his teeth together and, sweating thickly, stepped on. The elevator fell swift and deeper into darkness.

When it slammed to a stop, Jake looked around quickly. No one else was around . . . at least for the moment. He adjusted the strap of his bag against his shoulder and hustled down the hall. After a few wrong turns, he found it: the metal-framed doors that marked Andrew's chambers.

He took a deep breath, and then pounded as hard as he could. The sound of his knock echoed in the silence, but there was no answer. He waited, and then pounded again. And again. Finally, he glanced around the hall, and when he was sure it was empty, he started to yell.

"Denise!" he shouted, his voice breaking a little. "I know you're in there! Open up. Please! I need your help!"

The door slid open half an inch, and a darkly-shadowed eye peered out.

"They're gone, Jake!" she whispered, glancing down the hall anxiously.

"I know. You've got to tell me where."

Walking back to the elevator, he concentrated on being invisible. Luckily, he didn't see too many people in the halls, and he knew exactly where he was going. His stomach muscles relaxed as the doors slid open and he was back in the real world.

He stepped onto the metro and stood holding onto the rail as the train sped away, toward a more familiar corner of the world. He kept checking himself as it went.

Was he sure he could do this?

Sort of.

Was there any other way?

None that was fast enough.

I can do this, he said to himself, over and over. *I know what I have to do, and I can do it.*

But he still wasn't sure.

Jake stayed on the train and watched the surroundings outside the window grow shabbier. The graffiti got thicker and more vulgar on the buildings they sped past. The sidewalks were broken. When he stepped off onto the platform, Jake felt a shiver deep inside him. He couldn't help it. This place still felt like home.

He walked the streets confidently, not even needing to think about where he was going. He checked his watch. It was the right time of day.

Jerry was right where he knew he would find him, lounging under the same old lamp post. He smiled broadly when he saw Jake walk up.

"My old friend!" he hooted. "Where you been all this time? I've been looking 'round for you. I've got something you're really going to like!"

And there it was. Jake knew there would be drugs, knew that he'd have to come close to them, very close. But somehow it still took him by surprise, or at least his response to them did. It was like his body was a horse he was riding, but couldn't really control. It lurched toward the drugs, strained to be nearer to them, pulled instantly at every muscle, every sinew of his body.

He had never, ever, in his life, wanted anything so bad.

"Not today," Jake said. He had been planning to smile, to joke around. To make it look like it didn't cost him any effort. But there was no point. His body was sweating and groaning to escape from his control. His hands shook.

"I need something . . . different . . . today," he grunted.

Jerry looked at him strangely and slid the drugs back into his pocket. As soon as they were out of sight, Jake huffed out a breath between his teeth. He could see clearer.

"Okay," Jerry said slowly, his eyes narrowing a little. "What d'you need?"

"A gun," Jake said. "I need a gun."

MOLLY

Molly went back to the Refuge, fully aware that she was making a deal with the devil. She and Andrew might be on the same side, but now she knew that he could be ruthless, and cruel. And she was going to help him get his hands on something incredibly powerful.

She'd do a lot worse than that to make Jake well.

Whatever happened, whatever trouble Andrew made, she'd deal with it. Later. After Jake was safe.

Molly had worried about how she would explain Jake's absence, but Andrew didn't even seem to notice that Jake was gone—he was too wrapped up in planning and practicing, and getting everything ready for their try for the goblet.

Matt and Thia asked, but Molly evaded their questions. After trying a few times, they stopped asking, and instead became overly sympathetic, giving her big hugs and bringing burgers, fries, and once an entire apple pie to her room. They must have assumed that Jake was back on drugs, and gone for good. It was better that way, and safer for him. Still, Molly felt a little guilty as she ate the last crumb of the pie. She hadn't intended to deceive them.

She tried to just not think about Jake, which mostly didn't work. Still, time passed quickly. Andrew insisted on talking through every detail of his plan over and over, trying to make sure that she knew as much as possible about what would happen, and what she would need to do.

When the night of the full moon came, Molly was antsy and anxious to get on with it. No matter how things went, at least now she could be done talking about it.

"All ready?" Andrew asked when she met him in the hall. "It's time to get going. Let me introduce you to my friend, who will be coming with us. He's been a part of this search from the very beginning. We've been friends ever since we were kids. He was the one who was with me, back when we first found the tunnels that would one day become the Refuge." Andrew motioned to a man with scrubby red hair who smiled broadly and embraced Andrew like a brother. "Molly, meet Troy."

Shock rolled through Molly, hard and cold. She knew that name. She looked at Troy: the sneer on his face, the appraising disdain in his eyes. This was the man who had molested Evie.

This was Andrew's *friend*.

"Molly?" Andrew asked, staring at her. Molly realized that she had done nothing to hide the shock and horror on her face. "What's wrong?"

"H . . . he's a *Legacy*!" she stammered, saying the first thing she could think of that might sound plausible. "How can we trust him?"

Andrew laughed. "Oh, don't worry about that, Molly." He leaned over and whispered in her ear, "Troy's been after the goblet even longer than I have. His father passed him over for leadership of the family house. He wants a way to become more powerful just as badly as we do. Believe me."

"You sure she can do what you say she can?" Troy asked Andrew, his lips pressed together in a mocking expression. "She doesn't look like much."

"I know that Molly can do this, and with the two of us there to help her . . ." He shrugged. "This can really happen."

Troy snorted skeptically but didn't argue. They followed Andrew up the elevator and out of the metro station, to where a car was waiting. Andrew slid behind the wheel, and Troy took the seat across from him. Molly climbed into the back seat. The two of them launched into a conversation as though Molly wasn't even there, for which she was extremely grateful.

Bile kept rising in her throat, at the thought of sitting so close to someone she hated so much. They drove for hours. Molly stared out the window, watching as the full moon, trailed, watchful, just behind them.

The sun came up over the mountains and, even with her heart mired in darkness, Molly's breath caught at the beauty of it. Molly stared up at them as the car wound closer and closer to their destination. They stretched, gray and implacable, into the burgeoning sunshine. They seemed so ancient, so proud of the secret that they hid deep within.

When they climbed out of the van, she hurriedly pulled Andrew aside, going far enough away that she was sure Troy wouldn't overhear them.

"I know who Troy is, Andrew," she told him, "I know what he did to Evie. How can you be friends with that man?"

Andrew's face darkened. "I didn't realize," he said, his voice serious. "You have to understand, I don't approve of lots of things that Troy does, Molly. Any of them, really. Why do you think I helped Evie get away from her parents, and then hid her in the Refuge for so long?"

Molly blinked with surprise, and Andrew hurried to say more.

"Listen, he's a rotten person, and I know it. But I've known Troy since we were kids. I can control him."

"Listen," Molly ground her teeth, "I don't care if you guys rode bikes together in grade school. This guy is a monster. And you're talking about helping him become even more powerful!"

"I can control him!" Andrew whispered hurriedly. "He listens to me! I don't expect you to see the good in Troy. But the truth is, Molly, he is extremely powerful. His household is one of the oldest in the country. His Voice is born out of a thirteen-generation line. He's the one who got us all the documents about where the goblet is hidden." Andrew shrugged. "I know it isn't fun, or pretty, but once we get the cup . . . everything will be different." His eyes warmed as he thought of it, and he put a hand on Molly's shoulder. "Trust me, Molly. We can do this!" He rubbed her shoulder, as though she were an over-anxious child. "It'll work out. Come on."

Andrew took the lead, and Troy the rear. Molly did not fail to notice that they had boxed her in, but it made little difference. She had no thoughts of running. Both Troy and Andrew had silently pulled on packs as they departed the van. They took a long, rocky path, down to the very foot of one of the mountains. Molly was relieved that they were forced to walk single file and save their breath. She was trying very hard to think. Eventually, they reached the bottom, where the sand was still sodden, and several tiny shelled creatures flailed helplessly in the sand, left behind in the unforgiving sun when the tide pulled away.

"Right over here!" Andrew shouted, pointing to a small opening in the rock.

His voice was filled with its usual bravado, but he spoke somewhat breathlessly. Molly's eyes narrowed as she looked at him. He was sweating profusely, and his face was bright red.

"Are you ready?" Andrew asked her, grinning.

Molly grimaced, unable to feign the excitement that seemed to glow inside him. "Not at all," she answered grimly. "But if we're going to do this, then let's get it over with."

"Great," Andrew turned to Troy. "Listen," he said, lowering his voice slightly, as though saying something in great confidence, "I think the smart play here is for you to stay and guard the entrance," Andrew looked over his shoulder, as though Sirens might burst out of the bushes at any moment. "Molly and I will back soon. But we need someone to watch our backs."

Troy rocked back on his heels, his expression wary. "You wouldn't be thinking of double-crossing me, Andrew. Would you?" He asked, his eyes narrow.

"Are you kidding?" Andrew cried, flinging his arms out to the side. "Is that what you think? When the Watchers might come at any moment, and stop us before we even get a chance to start?" Andrew shook his head. "We need someone to stand watch. Besides," Andrew lifted a shoulder expressively. "You know as well as I do that this is risky. There's no telling what exactly might be in there. There's no reason for you to be exposed to the worst of the risk."

Troy nodded slowly, pursing his lips. "Hell," he said, "if you want to go climbing around in the dark without me, by all means: be my guest."

Andrew laughed and slapped Troy on the shoulder.

"We'll be back soon," he promised, and he and Molly walked toward the opening to the cave.

Just as they were about to step inside, Troy called after them. "Oh, and Andrew, I should just tell you one other thing."

"What?" Andrew asked, his voice uncertain.

Troy pulled a gun from where it had hung hidden, beneath his clothes. "I am prepared to defend you. But I'm also prepared to shoot you if you don't give me what's supposed to be mine," he grinned nastily, "old friend."

Andrew gave a forced laugh, as though Troy had said something funny. "See you soon," he repeated, then grabbed Molly's elbow, and pulled her with him into the cave.

"Great," she muttered, "now the maniac has a gun."

Andrew shrugged. "I figured he had one on him somewhere," he said. "Troy hordes weapons like a squirrel collects nuts."

"Maybe you don't have as much control over him as you like to think," Molly observed quietly.

They walked deeper into the cave. Molly had never been in darkness like this before. It seemed eager, the way it stretched out to the very edge of the doorway, reaching out for her. Only a few steps in, and already it was all around her, lying heavy on her skin and pressing, like a cool hand, against her forehead. Andrew had a large flashlight which he held in front of his chest like a talisman, swinging it back and forth, but the weak beam of light skirting across the gray rock only made the darkness around them seem thicker. They walked together deeper down the tunnel's throat. Molly reached out and touched the wall of stone beside her—it was perfectly smooth, cold, and slightly damp. Her foot slipped, and she looked down. The floor that they walked on was the same stuff – rock so sleek that it seemed to have been carefully polished. Molly wasn't sure if the moisture was from condensation or some other source. She was filled with a sudden apprehension. What if she slipped? What if she fell here, and slid ahead, alone, deeper and deeper into darkness?

They walked a few more steps before Molly realized that the tunnel was getting narrower as they went. She and Andrew had started out simply walking side by side, but now their shoulders pressed tight together. Another minute in and Andrew fell back to walk behind her, wordlessly placing a hand on her shoulder. The passageway was also shrinking from above, she had to crouch slightly to keep from bumping her head. Molly felt the stone closing in around her, and suddenly it was hard to breathe.

"How narrow is this going to get?" she asked Andrew, looking back around to see his face.

He shook his head, "We've just got to get through it. Keep going, Molly," and he gave her shoulder a small pat that was almost a shove. The air was stale here, and Molly could smell the damp and the mold.

Suddenly she stumbled as the ground changed. She was at the bottom of a twisting stairway. She looked back at Andrew, who was staring at the stairs, his brow furrowed. Molly noticed that he was sweating, and though they hadn't walked far yet, his chest was heaving as though he had just run a great distance.

"I don't know," he said, answering the question in her eyes. "I didn't see anything about a staircase in any of the documents I had. Nothing," he licked his lips and then motioned with his flashlight for her to begin the climb.

The stairway narrowed as it spiraled up and up, closing around them like a tightening fist. The air smelled of wet clay and still water, of things that festered and multiplied in the dark. In her ears, the silence whispered; and though Molly could not understand the words, still, deep inside, she trembled, and wished herself far, far away, to anyplace but this.

Later, she could not remember which of them it was who started screaming first.

They had reached what seemed, at last, to be the highest part of the stairs and stumbled, with tired, shuffling feet, onto a floor once more level and smooth as glass. Molly's legs throbbed, and the blood thrummed in her thighs. They were standing at the entrance to a long corridor that unfurled before them, dark and empty. The ceiling was so low that Molly felt it brush like velvet against the top of her head, catching in her hair like small, skeletal fingers.

Then something soft and warm touched her temple.

Tiny eyes blinked open, red and staring. There was just enough time to see wrinkled brown lips pulling back from bone white incisors, and to feel sharp bursts of wind press against their faces. Something hit Molly against her cheek and left a wet, warm trail of blood behind.

Then the screaming started.

It could have been Andrew, when he realized that the low ceiling was covered with living creatures, who hung upside down and gazed at him malevolently, eye to eye. Or it could have been Molly, who had suddenly felt that one of the leathery creatures had reached out and caught hold of her hair, and was pulling itself toward her. Or it could have been one of the creatures themselves, furious at the disturbance, or glorying that finally, after generations of waiting, the moment of their usefulness had come. But whatever its origin, a single, deep throated scream broke the silence.

And then came chaos.

The sound did not fade away, but hurled itself against one wall of the cave and then another, thrown back and forth, shattering and multiplying. The echoed scream grew and grew until it filled the cave, building in intensity until Molly found herself adding to the horrible noise, covering her ears and screaming in earnest from the pain that radiated through her eardrums. All around her bats were screaming in protest, waking and flying thick and wild through the cramped cave room, beating their wings in her face, hissing as they swung in front of her eyes. For long minutes Molly was lost in the wave of sound and the flurry of boney bodies swirling around her like angry bees. But then the bats were fewer, and the sound began to fade.

"Look," Andrew gasped, pointing, and Molly's eyes followed where he was pointing to. Hundreds and hundreds of bats sailed up, seeming almost elegant now that they weren't near, spiraling to where a small cleft in the rock opened up into a window. They flooded out into the sky.

"Oh, thank God that's over," Molly said, feeling her arms, where dozens of little scratches now crisscrossed the arms that she had held up in front of herself to shield her face.

"It isn't over," Andrew said, and his voice trembled. Molly spun around to stare, she had never heard fear in his voice before. "Don't you understand what just happened?" His face was bleeding too, and he mopped his bleeding forehead with the cleanest bit of his sleeve, "What do you think that was?" he waited for a minute, but Molly did not respond. He walked over to her and leaned in close, "We set off the *alarm.*" He glared at her, as though this was somehow her fault. "Just imagine what it is going to look like outside right now! Hundreds, maybe even thousands of bats swirling over the mountaintop. Like a giant smoke signal! The Watchers will see, and they will know that we're here. They will come for us." He walked away from her and leaned against the wall weakly, a hand over his face. "Shit. We've got to hurry. It's too late to go back, and I have no idea how soon they'll be able to get here." He adjusted the bag on his shoulders, a useless, nervous motion. "Come on!" he almost shouted, as though she had been holding them up.

"There," he whispered a moment later, as the passage began to broaden "That's the doorway. The guards will be just through there. Just use your voice to keep them still, and I'll take care of everything else, alright. Here we go . . ."

"Wait!" Molly whispered urgently. Andrew turned around, his eyes wide with confusion.

"Just . . . give me a minute," Molly said, forcing herself to breathe, trying to collect her thoughts. But the more she thought, the more she tried to calm herself, the more panicked she felt.

"Oh, never mind!" she exclaimed. "Let's just go!" And Molly rushed in front of Andrew, bursting into the chamber ahead.

JAKE

It was annoying not having a license. Not having a credit card. The world had boiled down to a few basic, shining truths for Jake. He wanted to keep only them in his mind. He wanted to focus on them completely, and not be distracted. It felt like the world ought to simplify around him, too. That it ought to be as straightforward as his own thinking. But it wasn't. There were train schedules and city maps. There were bus stops and foul-mouthed cabbies. Jake could hardly stand it. He had made his decision, had started on his plan. It seemed unbearable to stand in line at the train station. He felt like the world would end, and tumble down around his feet in smoldering, black chunks of destruction, if he had to wait one, more, fucking, minute, for his goddamned ticket.

He kept checking his watch, though that made it worse. He wanted it to be worse. He kept fingering his earlobe, and the tiny lines that were indented there forever. That made it worse, too. Like wading through deep water, he forced himself to wait for one train, and then another. He took a cab, a ferry, and two buses. And when he could get no farther on public transportation, he walked out to the forest and ran. He was closer, now. He stopped sometimes and checked his map. Denise had known everything, just as he knew she would. She had been very good at giving him directions. Now he could see the cliffs in the distance. He could hear the waves, not too far away.

He could smell the ocean.

The sunlight was pushing through the trees, making deep black shadows fall behind them. Jake stopped and stood, panting. It was time.

He had held guns before, but he had never fired one. It was already loaded, but Jake checked it carefully. He saw that his hand was shaking, and that worried him. It worried him a lot. This whole goddamned scheme of his bothered him, to be honest. What the fuck was he thinking? But he didn't stop.

He knelt down on the ground. It was still wet from the dew, he could feel the damp soaking into the knees of his pants. He held the gun in his hand, unsure of what to do.

He brought it up, slowly. He pointed it carefully, willing his hand to be steady, willing himself to be strong, and hold still. Not to flinch. The first shot was like a cannonball exploding, right next to his ear. It made the whole forest vibrate with the sound of silver bells ringing, but their music was only for Jake. He looked behind him into the trees after he fired, as though checking to make sure he hadn't hit something by mistake. There was nothing there but trees and wind and ringing silence. He moved the gun to the other side and fired again. It was so loud that it felt like someone was ramming him with a battering ram, hitting him solidly in the side of the face. His eyes watered like he had been cutting onions. But it wasn't enough. His ears rang, but when he snapped his fingers in front of his face, he could still hear it faintly. He ground his teeth together, closed his eyes tight, and did it again. And again. And again.

When he was done, he had used every single bullet that he had, and he couldn't hear a fucking thing.

Nothing.

The world had turned into a silent movie, and the grass didn't rustle as he stepped through it—the waves didn't whisper on the rocks. He looked up at the cliffs and got shakily to his feet.

He was ready.

BEA

They were both waiting when the King returned. He came in a boat of polished wood so beautifully crafted that, even with loss swelling inside her, Bea couldn't help but smile when she saw it. She ran her fingers across the wood, letting her fingers caress the smoothness of its sides.

They climbed aboard and, wordlessly, Malachai offered her a blanket. Bea wrapped it around her shoulders, noticing as she did so just how very thin she had become. Though the morning sun shone strongly, she was grateful for the warmth. Her angel stood next to the King in the prow. Bea did not look back at the lighthouse as the boat pulled out into the water. She felt it, rather than watched it, disappear behind her.

Bea closed her eyes and let her weariness fold in around her. She used it as a tool now, a defense against thought. She barely felt the boat moving. When she opened her eyes again, the mountains were all around her, gray and white. Snow-capped peaks loomed high above her. Seagulls cried in the distance. The sun was shining.

"Here," the King said. It was the first time anyone had spoken since they climbed aboard the boat. Bea looked and saw a narrow path, lined with white stones. It twisted up and around the side of the mountain. Her angel held her arm as they climbed on shore.

"There is a back way into the chamber," the King pointed up the path. "It has only one guard . . . one I selected and put in place myself." He turned to Bea. "He will admit you. You must retrieve the goblet and then bring it back here, to the water's edge, and drink."

Bea nodded silently.

"Would you like Malachai to hold you, Bea? We could fly up if you wish."

Bea shook her head slowly. "No," she said. "I can walk."

Her angel held her hand as they climbed. His hand squeezed hers over and over, as though each time he loosened his hold, he realized how little time he had left to hold her, and had to tighten his grip.

The King seemed, after a time, to grow agitated. He kept glancing up the path ahead of them and back at the boat below, as though measuring again and again just how far they had come, and finding their progress much, much too slow. Bea ignored his anxiety. She was no baby, to be carried from place to place. Besides, the day was beautiful, the air was fresh. Bea wanted the walk, the feel of the dirt under her feet, the way the wind made her pants billow around her thin legs. The path narrowed, and they were forced to walk single file, the King leading the way.

"I think I will fly up, and measure the distance we have left to travel," the King said at last, launching himself in the air and circling over them once before flying toward the top of the mountain.

Bea looked up, her eyes following his movement in the air. Just then, a black cloud erupted from a hidden opening in the mountain's side. Bea gasped. The cloud moved like a living thing, contracting and expanding, swirling upward.

The King pulled up short in the air, and even at a distance, Bea could see the shock spread across his face, as he hovered there, staring at what Bea now realized were hundreds of bats streaming up into the sky together.

The King turned around, his wings beating furiously as he dived toward them.

The shot came out of nowhere.

The sound of it shattered the silence, whizzing through the air, unbelievable. Impossible. But it was there.

A small cloud of feathers floated behind the King, where the bullet had shot through his wing. He dipped in the air, flapping his wings frantically, trying to steady himself in the air. Blood fell from his wound like red rain.

Malachi was frozen, staring above, just a few feet away from her. Bea saw his whole body convulse, saw a tremor run through him as he tensed, and his chest swelled. Suddenly, Bea knew her danger. She lurched forward, tripping over her own feet as she fell forward, grabbing desperately at his arm. At her touch Malachai jerked, and his eyes cleared. Instantly, his chest deflated, the cry that had instinctively risen to his lips falling away. Now, instead, he looked around him wildly. Bea understood. His voice was his one true weapon, and he could not use it with her near.

Her angel bent his knees and shot up into the air, rushing to help his king.

"No!" Bea screamed, her voice shattering as she called after him. "They'll just shoot you too!" But he ignored her, and seconds later he was at the King's side, pulling his arm around his shoulder and supporting him as they descended through the air.

A second shot rang through the air.

"NO!" Bea screamed helplessly. But the shot had gone wide, and seconds later the King and Malachai were collapsing on the ground.

"It is a minor wound," the King grunted, stretching out his wing so that he could see the ragged hole. "It will heal quickly, in the Moon Pool. But they are here." He cursed quietly in a language

Bea did not understand. "We are too late to avoid a confrontation."

"But they're going through the front way, right?" Bea asked.

The King nodded grimly.

"Then I can still beat them to it."

The King looked at her doubtfully, and Bea straightened up.

"I can do it," she insisted.

The King nodded. "Very well," he said. "I must go and summon the others. You and Malachai continue on, and I will return as soon as I can."

"No," Bea said forcefully, and both the King and her angel froze, turning slowly to look at her. But Bea was looking only at the King.

"You're too weak to fly by yourself. I can do this on my own."

"You are sure?" The King asked, even as Malachai shook his head at her, his eyes pleading.

"Yes. I would just ask one thing from you, in return for what I am doing."

Worry flashed across the King's face. "What service can I do for you?" he asked, uncertainly.

"Keep him safe," Bea said, her voice breaking as she motioned toward her angel. "Take him with you. Keep him away from the danger. If I try to do this thing, even if I fail, I want your word that you'll still do everything in your power to protect him from harm."

The King stood, though Bea could tell the movement pained him.

"You have my oath," he said, inclining his head slightly. "It is well asked, and gladly given."

Bea nodded to him, and wordlessly she turned and lay a hand against Malachai's chest. He looked down at her. There were no words.

"Go," she said, backing away from them, but not quite able to look away. "Get out of here!"

She saw the King reach out, placing a hand on Malachai's arm to keep him from following her. With a wrench of will, she forced herself to turn and charge up the mountainside. She did not look back again.

She ran, though she was not well enough for running. Her body screamed and beat its fists in protest, punching awareness of pain against her consciousness again and again. Bea ignored it. She had decided to do this . . . she had laid in for this course. She fell once, and a jagged rock cut deep into her shoulder. She ignored it, paid no attention to the blood that seeped down her front, pushing herself up and forcing herself to run again.

Soon she could see it, a dark cleft in the rock that looked like a doorway. She felt a wave of relief seep through her.

It disappeared when she saw the man with the machine gun.

He was huge and thick with muscles, his hair cropped close to his head in a military style. He held the machine gun in his hand, pointing it directly at Bea's chest. She stopped and stood, looking at him. She had never had a gun pointed at her before, and the man held it steadily, his finger wrapped around the trigger. He would not flinch at killing her, would hardly remember that he had done it.

Bea felt no fear at all.

"Who sends you?" he asked.

Bea paused. This was the guard that the King had spoken of, but he had not told her that there would be questions.

"I send myself," she said quickly, hoping that she would get the answers right. "I am coming to get the cup, to destroy it before it can be used by others."

The man stared at her, evaluating her. He did not lower the gun.

"And are you whole, and unbroken?" he asked.

Bea laughed. She couldn't help it. She looked helplessly down at herself, at her bloodstained clothing, her thin, brittle limbs.

"I am sick," she said, "and dying. My breasts have been sliced off, my head shaved. I am in pain, and I am rushing toward a death I do not want. But, yes. I am whole. I am unbroken."

The man nodded.

"I can hear your freedom in your voice," he said, as he lowered his gun and stepped aside. "Go quickly, then. I cannot leave my post, not even to help you."

"Thank you," Bea said, slipping past him quickly.

She felt the closeness of the end now. Felt it pulling her, like a dream that calls you back when you aren't really quite awake.

The passageway was dark and so narrow that Bea could feel the ceiling, hovering just a few inches above her head. The floor was paved with stones, but the wall and arcing ceiling were nothing but earth, wet and damp and fragrant.

She ran.

MOLLY

There was a moment of total silence.

A hundred pairs of eyes . . . no, more . . . two hundred . . . more . . . in a single instant were all burning into Molly. The shock held them still. For one moment, the impossibility of her presence, the audacity of it, kept them from responding. And for that same instant, the sight of them held Molly utterly still.

They barely looked human.

Skin so pasty white that she knew with certainty that it had been years since any of them had seen the sun. Limbs emaciated, sticking like dry white bones out from inside clothing that billowed around them grotesquely. And their eyes . . . Molly stared into them like a person might stare into a bottomless pit.

"My God," she had just enough time to think, "what has happened to these people?"

Then, as one, she saw them all reaching for their weapons. Hundreds of guns, one for each skeleton-like defender, began to rise to point right at her chest.

Molly closed her eyes.

Andrew had told her not to, had cautioned her to maintain eye contact with the guards . . . but she didn't care. Because when she closed her eyes, she could see Jake's face.

She began to sing.

The words she chose did not matter . . . she couldn't really control so many at once. She could only hope to keep them still, to hold them in place. If it worked, Andrew would hurry around the room, subduing them one by one, as quickly as possible. If it didn't work, she'd find out when the first bullet hit.

She closed her eyes, and suddenly Jake was smiling up at her from just in front of the stage. She looked down at him, and the music tumbled out of her. He understood every word. He nodded with the rhythm, his eyes melting with emotion that surged back and forth between them, the music an electric current in the air. She looked into his eyes, and there she saw herself reflected, exactly as she wished to be. She saw herself as a poet, an angel. She saw herself as powerful, her words a sword that held all the shadows at bay. She did not look around her, but she sang and sang. The sound echoed off the walls of the cave, echoing, multiplying the sound. It reverberated in the stone around them, making her eardrums quiver. It was so loud. She covered her ears, trying to hear the words from inside her head, rather than from outside. She finished one song and began another. Still, she did not look. She had not died yet and felt a small flare of relief, but quickly squelched it. No matter how many she held still . . . it would only take one shot to kill her.

Time stopped. There was only darkness, and Jake's face, and music. At one point it occurred to Molly to wonder if she had died without realizing it and slipped into her own version of eternity. For a moment she almost opened her eyes to check, but then decided not to. She wasn't ready to know.

When Andrew's hand came down on her shoulder, she stumbled from the impact, even though his touch was feather-light.

"It's over!" he hurried to tell her, reaching out to support her when her knees gave out. "They're no threat to us now."

Cautiously, Molly opened her eyes. The first thing she saw was guns. All the guns that Andrew had stripped from the guards as they stood, immobile, and tossed aside. The second thing she saw was bodies. The cavern was full of them.

"Are they . . ." she whispered.

"No! Of course not!" Andrew hurried to assure her. "Just tied up."

Molly stared at them. Hundreds of prone forms, lying with their hands bound behind them, still held immobile by the last fading echo of her song.

"I couldn't have done it alone," Molly admitted. "I couldn't have done more than hold them still."

No," Andrew replied seriously, looking around him in awe. "I can hardly believe that you managed what you did."

A scream broke the silence. Two screams. A dozen. Suddenly the cavern echoed with an endless, horrible symphony of agony. One by one, as the guards awoke from the trance that Molly had pulled them into, they began to writhe, to roll back and forth, to moan deep, guttural cries of despair.

"What's wrong with them?" Molly cried, covering her ears and ducking down, as though she could block the sound by getting closer to the ground. It was the loudest, most heart-breaking thing she had ever heard. "What did you do to them?"

"Nothing!" Andrew yelled, straining to be audible over the horrible din. "It wasn't me. It's their bond, to their Singers! They realize that they've failed!" His eyes combed the room, but the revulsion that Molly felt was not mirrored in his eyes. His eyes were full of awe. "Just look at them!" he said with wonder.

Molly looked.

Just a few feet from her a man lay on his stomach. He was muscular or had been once, though now his arms looked brittle. He was middle-aged, his brown hair streaked with gray and stained from the thick dust that covered the cavern floor. He stared up at Molly, but his eyes didn't really see her. Molly watched, frozen, as tears filled the eyes of this big man who was old enough to be her father. His body began to shake, and then he began to sob great, unguarded sobs. Sobs that ought to belong to a child. Tears ran down his face and then, suddenly, he roared in despair and began to beat his forehead against the stone floor. Molly screamed as the rock beneath him turned red. He lifted his head and howled, and the sound belonged to a wounded animal. Not a man.

"Come on," Andrew urged, grabbing her hand and pulling her through the writhing figures, toward an opening at the back of the cavern.

"We can't leave them like this!" Molly cried. "We have to help them!"

"Nothing we can do," Andrew said firmly, his fingers tightening around her wrist. "This is who they are. They are bound too tightly with their Singers." He glanced back, and the horror in Molly's eyes finally registered. "Don't worry about it!" he said firmly. "They'll be fine."

He pulled her down into a narrow, dark hallway. Their path turned, and the sound was muffled. But Molly could still hear them. She wondered if she would hear them, in her dreams, for the rest of her life. Andrew was ahead of her now, his eagerness pressing him forward even as Molly's feet dragged to a stop.

"We've done it!" Molly could hear him muttering to himself. "Holy shit! I can't believe we've done it." But there was no room in Molly's mind for victory.

Suddenly, she understood.

The hallway suddenly gave way to a large opening. A room carved from stone, a pedestal set in its center. A small fire burned in the corner, and orange-gray fire bathed the stone goblet in swatches of shadow and light.

"There it is." Andrew's voice was strangled with wonder. "It's really ours." He set his flashlight down on the floor and began to walk toward it.

"This . . . this is the cure you promised me?" Molly said, her voice a little more than a whisper. But something about it made Andrew stop and turn to her, staring. She met his gaze sadly. "You really thought I would want that? That I would want to do that . . . to Jake?" She shook her head in disbelief. "How could you think that?"

"You want him healed," Andrew said. "Now you can make him better."

"This wouldn't make him better, Andrew. It would take away who he is! This would wipe him away. You saw those people. You saw their eyes! They aren't there anymore . . . they aren't themselves. Why would I want to do that to someone I loved?"

Andrew's face flushed. "You don't understand what you're talking about," he said. "I know what we just saw was upsetting, but it won't always be like that. Those people out there . . . they are usually happy. Blissful. They have a kind of peace of mind that we can't even imagine."

"Did that look like peace of mind to you?" Molly's voice grew louder. "This is wrong, Andrew. This is a power that we aren't meant to have. If we use it on the people we love, we'll just destroy them. And ourselves." She reached out, as though to put her hand on his shoulder. "We can't do this. We have to stop."

Andrew raised his eyebrows. "This isn't your decision, Molly," he said. "If you've decided you don't want to drink from the goblet, then you're a fool, but I won't force you. But you don't decide for me."

He turned away from her and took a step toward the goblet.

"Stop, Andrew."

Andrew froze without turning around.

"Don't make me challenge you, Andrew. Please. Just walk away with me now. This doesn't have to turn into a fight."

Andrew snorted. "You're afraid of losing," he said, an unfamiliar sneer in his voice.

"No," Molly said, sadly. "Not anymore."

Something in the air snapped, and suddenly Andrew was on top of her, and the small stone room filled up with shouts and screams and wordless grunts. Their voices echoed against the walls of the cave, and blended with the screams that still sounded just down the corridor, and a sound . . . like a gunshot, that came from somewhere outside. But as Andrew yelled down at her, Molly found that something inside her had changed. She mourned for him as she overcame him, but overcoming him was not hard. The place inside her where her voice lived was no longer far below the surface; it smoldered inside her, ready and eager to burst into flame. Her throat burned as she yelled back at Andrew, her voice cutting across his, drowning him out, stunning him with its force. She saw the agony in his eyes as he realized what was happening, as his eyes turned toward the goblet, so close, but suddenly forever out of reach.

There was a snap when it happened, a tremor in the air.

She felt the moment when her will broke through, sensed the fissure somewhere deep inside his core. For a split second everything was in slow motion: the pain that lit up Andrew's face, the way his eyes rolled back and his knees gave out. Then, suddenly, it was over. Andrew lay unconscious on the ground, and the only sound was the echo of the screams that still reverberated on the cavern's walls.

Molly averted her eyes from Andrew's prone form as she stepped around him and picked up the goblet. It was strange to hold it, bizarre to think of what it could do. Its thinly carved green stone glinted, and it felt so light, so fragile in her hand.

The moment that she touched it, the goblet filled with red liquid, the surface of it glimmering strangely.

At first, Molly thought that the simple pressure of her fingers would be enough to break it into bits. She lifted the goblet high above her head and threw it full force against the cave's stone wall.

With a thick thud that did not at all match its delicate appearance, the goblet clanged against the ground. Unharmed.

"Dammit!" Molly cursed quietly. She picked it up and threw it again. And again.

Not a chip in the stone, not a dent in the cup's untroubled face.

Molly began to sweat. What if she couldn't get rid of it? She smashed the cup against the pedestal it had come from. Nothing helped.

"You can't destroy it that way."

Molly's heart stuttered. She spun around, to find a pale, thin face emerging from the dark.

BEA

"You can't destroy it that way."

Bea stepped out of the shadows and into the room. The woman froze.

They stared at each other. Somehow, this woman seemed familiar to Bea, as though she had seen her before, hundreds of times, in a crowd, so that seeing her now wasn't really a surprise. It felt expected that the woman would push a strand of hair out of her eyes and say in a strained voice, "Who are you?"

"It won't work," Bea said again. "It can't just be broken."

"What do I do with it, then?" the woman said, as though to herself, holding the cup out and away from her body. Distancing herself from it. She glanced at the door apprehensively, and Bea understood that she was not alone and that she was afraid of whoever might be coming.

"Give it to me." Bea stepped forward and held out her hand. "That's what I've come for."

The woman took a distrustful step back. "Tell me how," she said. "I'll do it."

"Listen to my voice." Bea was beginning to grow anxious. "I'm not . . ." Bea found she had no words for what she was trying to say, "I'm not like you are. I can't use the cup for myself. Do you believe me?"

The woman nodded, slowly.

"Then give it to me." Bea held out her hand. "It has to be me."

"Why?" The woman hesitated, her hand still tight around the goblet. "Why can't I do it?"

"Because," Bea snapped, exasperated, "I'm the one who's supposed to die today."

The woman looked at Bea. Her face paled, as understanding sunk in.

"Give it to me," Bea said steadily, and Molly walked over and put the goblet in her hand.

They looked at each other steadily for a long moment. Bea saw no pity in the woman's eyes, only admiration. Somehow that made her feel glad.

She nodded in wordless thanks, and then spun around and fled toward the passageway, leaving the strangely familiar woman behind her.

She had just entered the darkness when she heard an explosion of sound behind her.

"What the fuck is going on here?" a man's voice roared, echoing in the tiny passageway. "What have you done to Andrew?"

"It's gone, Troy," the woman's voice answered. "Help me carry Andrew. We've got to just turn around and get out."

Bea could hear feet crunching over stone.

"Two of those dammed Watchers sailed by just now," the man was saying. "I took a shot at them . . . damn near took one of them down."

Bea stiffened. This was the man who'd tried to kill her angel. She took a step back toward the cavern and peered back into the cave.

"They'll be back soon, and the only way we can stand up to them is if we can do everything that they can." He stood, towering over the woman. He didn't need to threaten her—he was a threat, his whole body a punch just pulled, a hammer waiting to fall on anyone who came within its reach. He bristled with power like a rabid dog on a short leash.

"Where is it, Molly? Tell me."

Molly smiled up at him.

"Make me," she said.

Howling with sudden rage, he flew at her.

Bea turned and began to run.

Behind her, she could hear blows, the sound of flesh pounding against flesh. The kind-eyed woman screamed, and Bea ran faster.

Soon she saw that the darkness was fading to a cheerless gray, and then the sunlight called to her from the entrance of the passageway. She sped past the watchman, who made no comment as she fled. She ran, full-out, down the mountainside. The ocean seemed so far away, but soon, faster than she would have thought possible, she felt wet sand under her bare feet, felt the water lap against her toes.

There was no time to think, and Bea did not want to.

She did not stop, or look around. She held the cup up, staring down at the strange red liquid that filled it to the brim, fascinated and repulsed by the way it glowed in the sunshine. Then she brought it to her lips and drank.

The cup was alive.

Bea hadn't realized it till it touched her lips, not until she felt it melt into her skin. The liquid should have been gone. She had choked and sputtered; she had drunk and drunk and drunk . . . but still it poured down her throat, burning her insides, pouring acid into her gut. The cup would not let go. It wanted to make her powerful . . . it would not stop until it felt her ability surge. It clutched at her.

But there was nothing in her for the goblet's power to latch onto. Bea felt her insides melting. She clawed at it with her fingernails, trying desperately to pry the thing off her face.

It hurt.

Hurt, hurt, hurt.

She wrestled with it, head thrown back, sunlight streaming down on her, till she felt like she would tear the skin of her face . . . anything.

And then it was over.

The goblet shuddered and cracked. Its pieces fell into the water and floated away, drained of all its power, drained of life. It had poured everything into Bea, and Bea stood motionless, knee deep in the water, eyes screwed shut.

For one split second, she felt nothing at all.

Then the pain came, and the blood boiled as it poured from her lips, steaming when it hit the water. Blood streamed from her nose, leaked like tears from her eyes. It was agony, agony, beyond agony. After just a few seconds, she had forgotten who she was. She had no name, no past. She knew nothing and was nothing, but a pulsation of pain that writhed in the water.

"I hate you," she screamed in her mind, though the pain and the blood silenced her. "God. I hate you. You asked this of me, and I did it. But don't think that I forgive you."

Then a wave, tall and green, rose up and smashed itself against the shore. Bea felt it hit her, felt its fingers wrap around her wrist. She did not kick or pull away this time. She let herself fall forward, let the tide pull her out to sea.

MOLLY

His voice did not have much effect on her. Molly was pleased by that, despite the pain. She had become powerful enough, at least, that when Troy yelled at her to choke, screamed at her to fall face down on the floor, the words rolled off her effortlessly.

It still wasn't enough. Her commands did next to nothing to him. There was no way that she could make him stop hitting her, nothing she could do about the force of his body, all taut muscle and practiced fists, as he fell on top of her. She fought back, glad when her knee found his groin, and she felt the ripple of pain run through him, happy when her fist connected with something deep and hollow in his stomach. But she was tired; and when he finally managed to knock her to the floor, she fell and lay stunned, feeling with calm certainty that she was about to die.

Until Jake ran in.

It was impossible. A dream. A hallucination brought on by hurt and worry, and the closeness of death. Except that a dream could not have punched Troy so powerfully from behind, in the side of the head. A hallucination could not have caused that shower of red to come spraying from Troy's nose, as he spun to meet his attacker.

"Trash!" Troy yelled, as though the insult of a Bloodbound challenging him was worse than the pain. "You think you can touch me, dog? *GET DOWN!*"

It should have been over.

Just those two words, spoken with such force and derision that even Molly felt herself shudder. Jake should have been on his knees. But he did not even slow. He threw himself at Troy, and Molly heard a bone crunch as Jake's fist connected with his face.

It was impossible.

Molly pushed herself up as well as she was able, watching, unbelieving, as Jake pounded into Troy, over and over.

"Stop!" Troy yelled, his face red with shock and blood, as Jake knocked him to the floor and fell on top of him. *"Get off me!"* He wasn't even trying to use his fists. The apparent uselessness of his voice scared Troy in a way that nothing else could, and that fear destroyed him. He fought only with his voice, and his voice did absolutely no good. Molly winced at the wet sound of fist against flesh that should have been firm but wasn't. Again and again Jake hit him, not stopping till Troy lay, motionless and stained with his own blood, on the ground.

"Jake!" Molly cried. He hurried to her, crouching down beside her and embracing her tightly.

"How . . . What are you doing here?" Molly asked in wonder.

Jake pulled away and looked at her. "I had to come after you," he said. "Denise told me where."

"I can't believe it," Molly said, reaching up and touching his cheek. "You saved my life. But you shouldn't have come . . . Are you alright?"

Jake didn't answer.

"Are you alright?" Molly asked again and felt a ripple of worry. Something was wrong.

Jake shook his head, and half-smiled.

"I can't hear you." He gestured to his ears. "I can't hear anything at all."

Molly stared at him in shock. She reached up and touched the side of his face. Her fingers came away covered in blood.

"What did you do to yourself?" she gasped.

"It's okay, Molly," he whispered. "It doesn't matter."

"It does!" Molly protested, and even though he couldn't hear her, he understood.

He shook his head, and he took her hand in his. "It was worth it," he said gently. "To me, you're worth everything. I had to come. You were right, Molly. Right about me. I can fight, after all." He smiled ruefully. "But I need you with me. You're my reason for fighting."

Molly smiled up at him, and Jake leaned down to take her in his arms.

A shot exploded, shaking the walls, making the air around them vibrate. Molly felt pain pierce her arm, looked down and saw red spilling from her shoulder.

"You're hurt!" Jake grunted. His voice sounded strangled.

"No, it's okay. It just grazed me."

Molly looked up. It was only then that she saw the small round hole in his chest.

It wept blood.

Such a small thing. Such a small, red circle. Just big enough to rip all the hope and joy from Molly's world.

Jake was looking down at it, too, and when their eyes met, he lifted up his hands. There was no shock on his face. Not even pain. Just a look of tiredness, and exasperation.

"I tried," his eyes said to her. "I did everything I could."

Even before his eyes had closed, Molly saw the darkness wash over him. She only just managed to catch him as he fell face forward toward the floor.

Molly had never known fear until that moment. Never known sorrow, or grief. All the emotions she had experienced up until now had been shadows, reflections a thousand times distilled.

Weightless.

They meant nothing, were worth nothing. Now was the first time she had ever felt the full weight of sorrow, and her heart burst open at the seams as it stretched its arms wide, and tried to hold it.

"Jake!" she screamed, and in her voice, at that moment, every ounce of power that she had ever felt, every moment of pain, of joy . . . every song she'd ever sung, came boiling to the surface, and her voice rang, beautiful and terrible in the same instant.

"Don't!" she screamed. *"Don't* leave me!"

Troy had pushed himself up from the ground unnoticed, and now limped toward her, his gun pointing at her. He leered at her, as though he could frighten her. As though the gun gave him some kind of power . . . he didn't understand that he could do nothing worse to her now. Molly was hardly aware of his presence. For her, the whole universe had shrunk down to the hand she held to Jake's throat, trying to tell if his heart was still beating.

But even through the fog of that panic, something reached Molly. And Troy, too. He looked up, away from her. Suddenly frightened. In a single instant, all the screaming and wailing in the outer cavern ceased.

Silence filled the cave.

EVIE

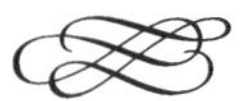

She opened her eyes, and everything felt unfamiliar.

The bed she was lying on felt strangely lumpy. Her hair lay in a tangled mass over her eyes. For a moment, she remembered absolutely nothing.

"Evie," she whispered to herself after a moment. That was her name. Or had been? Or would be? Everything seemed so fuzzy.

It was coming back, but for some reason, her memories were playing slowly, jerkily, like outdated black and white films. Evie pushed herself up to sitting and immediately pitched face forward, barely catching herself before she fell face forward off the bed. There was a lot of weight behind her that she wasn't used to maneuvering. Without thinking, Evie put her hand behind her.

Her fingers touched leather, smooth and warm.

"Oh!" Memory rushed back to her, and Evie stood up, staring around her in confusion. Her wings rose up behind her, spreading out of their own accord. It was only then that she noticed the small form sprawled on a pile of blankets by her bedside. The child with long black hair and night-black wings sat up and rubbed her eyes wearily.

"You have awakened," she commented, smiling, though her voice not quite managing to be cheerful. "It is early."

Evie stared at the girl wordlessly.

"I am Nomi," the girl explained. "My father sent me to keep you company till you woke."

"Your voice is so beautiful!" Evie said wonderingly.

Nomi smiled more earnestly and tucked her hair behind her ears. "Thank you," she said. "My father has always said so."

"Am I . . ." Evie looked around her, confused. She was trying so hard to remember. It had all seemed so clear before . . .

"You are not hurt," Nomi said firmly, taking her hand and gently pushing her back to sit on the bed. "Remember? You are one of our own people, now. You don't have to be frightened of my voice . . . it cannot harm you."

"Not at all?" Evie asked softly, embarrassed to sound so much like a child, but Nomi didn't seem to notice.

"Not at all," she said firmly. "Only the King's voice is powerful enough to impose his will on another of our kind. Now," she said, looking at Evie in a very businesslike way, "How are you faring? The transformation took all the energy out of you, and you have slept for three days. I'm sure that it is confusing."

"Three days?" Evie shook her head. "All I remember is coming out of the water and . . . and I . . ." She looked at Nomi with dawning wonder on her face. "I flew!"

"Yes," Nomi said, her voice a little clipped. "Even when we tried to call you back. You ignored us. We were all so afraid that you would fall!"

"But I didn't?" Evie said, trying to make her words sound like a statement, rather than a question, though in truth she didn't remember coming down at all.

"No," Nomi admitted it grudgingly. "Father would have called to you, but then you would have fallen for certain."

"Really?"

"Ummhmm." Nomi looked a little smug as she nodded; after

all, the King was her father. "It isn't just for show that everybody falls on their faces in front of him. His voice is . . . powerful. Anyway, I need to get you some food. You are hungry, are you not?"

Evie's hands fell to her stomach. It felt hollow and, now that she thought of it, aching.

Nomi nodded wisely. "Always the same with you Newbies. You always wake up starving after the change."

"Do you do this often?" Evie asked, her voice climbing several octaves.

"In the last century, counting you, we have done this exactly twice. Twice in the last year, actually. I think Father's getting a little soft-hearted. You stay here, and I'll bring you something."

A few moments later Nomi bustled back into the room, baring a small round platter heaped with food. Evie took it and ate from it, and for a moment they sat together in companionable silence.

"What is that?" Nomi said, rising from where she had been sitting against the wall and moving to peer out the window. "I can't imagine why they are making so much noise . . ."

Then Evie saw her whole body tense, and her wings spread out defensively behind her.

"Oh, no!" she cried. "It's Father!" She was gone in an instant, streaking out the door and down the hallway. Evie hurried to follow.

By the time she got outside, a crowd had gathered. Evie hung back, watching as Nomi pushed through the crowd toward her father, who was being supported by everyone who could get a hand close enough to hold him. His face was pained, and his white feathers were stained with red. Nomi stood, pressing her father's hand to her forehead while tears coursed down her cheeks.

"Who has dared to wound you, Father?" she asked, the formal words doing nothing to diminish the emotion in her voice. "Tell me who they are, so that I may lay them at your feet, to serve you forever in payment for their crime!"

"We will go and seek them, daughter. Do not worry. But first I must heal. The wound tears when I try to fly and Malachai has had to support me." It was only then that Evie noticed that they were standing at the side of the same pool, shaped like a teardrop, that she had found healing in just nights before.

"Simon! Oriel! I have need of you," the King called, and two of the Watchers separated from the crowd and presented themselves to the King. "You must stand guard, while I am in the waters," the King said, his voice rough with pain. "You must ensure that Malachai does not stir from this spot."

"My King!" Malachai cried, but the King ignored him. "Restrain him physically, if my command is not enough." The two nodded, and though they shot confused glances at each other, they did not question the King.

"Please, my Lord!" Malachai protested, and the King turned to him.

"I have given my word," he said wearily. "You will stay at my side until I am sure the danger has passed."

Malachai bowed his head and did not speak again as the King went and lowered himself into the pool. Evie saw that, just as it had for her, the surface of the pool immediately crusted over, sealing the King inside its healing waters. Nomi knelt by its side, leaning close so that she could glimpse her father's form through the cloudy shell. Malachai stood with a guard on either side of him, shoulders slumped. A moment later Evie noticed silent tears running down his face.

Not knowing why, she found herself inching closer to him. There was something strangely familiar about his face, his shoulder-length blonde hair...

"It's you!" she cried, shock running through her. "You're Roman's brother!"

Malachai looked up at her, and at first, his eyes did not focus. Then he saw her and stood up a little straighter.

"The girl from class?" he said, confused. "And you are one of us now?" His face clouded with confusion, and just at that moment, there was a great cracking sound.

She turned to see the King pushing himself out of the shell that covered the surface of the water.

"Gather every member of my personal guard to me!" he roared as he stepped, dripping, from the pool. "Now! We go NOW!" Evie shrank back from him, moving so that she was concealed behind a pillar. The sound of his fury made her tremble. "Evie, you too must accompany us."

"Evie has only just awakened, Father!" Nomi protested. "She will barely have the strength to fly!"

"That girl is stronger than you know, daughter." The King's voice softened as he looked down at Nomi. "And for her own sake, she must come."

Before Evie knew what was happening, she was flying through the air, surrounded by furiously beating wings. The thirty members of the King's personal guard were arrayed around him in the air, muscular men with fury in their eyes, and a few wiry women with weapons strapped to their sides. Malachai flew just a little behind them, his two guards still flanking him. As they flew, the King shouted to them, giving them instructions, explaining what they might find and what they must do. Evie tried to understand, tried to process all the information he called over to her, but her mind still felt halting and confused.

And then there were caves, and stone walls, and the sounds of hundreds of people wailing and flailing on the ground. The King led the way into the chamber, and for a second all of them stood, frozen in horror, looking at what had been done to their servants. The wriggling figures on the floor all turned, crying out, craning their heads to look up at the King.

"Shhhhhhhh," he whispered to them gently, and immediately they were all perfectly still. Their faces slackened, and peace filled their eyes. "Come," the King said, his voice barely audible, motioning to his guards. As he had commanded, Evie fell to the back, where she had been ordered to stay hidden in shadow.

The room that they entered seemed to be filled with wax figures, the four forms that they found there held motionless by the sight that suddenly burst in on them. Evie pulled up short, stopping just inside the entrance of the cave, feeling her whole body tremble.

She knew these people.

She had been expecting Steele to be standing there, his greedy fingers already tight around the goblet. Instead, she saw Molly, bleeding and covered in dirt, crouching over Jake's motionless form. The ground beneath Jake's body was stained with red. Just a few feet away, Andrew lay unconscious, his face slack, his fingers stretched out toward the empty pedestal where the goblet ought to have been.

And there was another man.

Evie froze. For a moment her heart did not beat, her mind could not function. She waited for the fear to flood her limbs, for terror to seize her, but it did not come. Her body was different now. She was different. Of their own accord, her wings lifted, tensed. Preparing to swoop. Her lips pulled back in a deadly, curving smile from her newly-sharpened teeth.

In place of fear, power. In place of terror, blood-lust.

Somehow the King knew. He turned, and though he spoke to them all, his eyes looked right into the shadows, to where Evie stood unseen.

"Only I will speak," he said. "I will find out all that has happened here. Only then, will we act." He raised an eyebrow at Evie, and she jerked herself up, out of a crouch she had unknowingly bent into, forcing her wings to settle behind her. She bowed her head, ever so slightly, to the King.

He turned to Troy, who stood with a gun held dumbly in the air before him. "Drop that ridiculous weapon," the King said softly, and the sound of the gun banging against stone echoed loudly through the chamber.

"It was her!" Troy cried, pointing toward Molly. "She and her slave came to steal the goblet from you!"

The King smiled menacingly, the whiteness of his teeth flashing in the firelight. "The goblet. Where is it?"

"Molly has it!" Troy stabbed his finger in Molly's direction, his eyes wild. "She's the one you want."

Slowly, the King turned, bringing the full force of his gaze on Molly.

"Where is it?" he repeated.

"I gave it to that woman." Molly looked straight into the King's eyes as she spoke and, though her face was stained with tears, her voice was steady. "I tried to destroy it, but I couldn't do it. The woman told me she could, so I gave it to her." Molly gestured to a small crevice in the back of the wall. "She took it and ran."

Malachai made a low moaning sound, deep in his throat. He spun and flung himself toward the opening, nearly evading the grasp of his guards, who seized him by the arms and wrestled him back. The King ignored the disturbance.

"Are there any more of you?" he asked icily. "If you lie to me, child, it will fall heavy upon you."

Molly shook her head. "No," she whispered. "Only us."

The King turned to where Malachai was struggling to pull free from the hands that held him back.

Release him," the King commanded. He looked at Malachai, and his eyes were full of sorrow. "Go to her," he said softly. Malachai fled.

The King turned his attention back to Troy. "I must have some words with you, Troy," the King said, folding his hands in front of him.

"I've done nothing wrong. I was only trying to stop them!"

"And yet you fired at me before," the King pointed out calmly, and all the color drained from Troy's face. "Did you think I could not see you?" The King's face hardened, and his smile turned predatory. "I see many things, Troy. And I know a great deal about you." His voice dropped, and Evie shivered. He seemed even more dangerous when he spoke so softly.

"You have spilled Siren blood. You have forced your way into our most protected chambers and tried to take what was never meant to be yours. Your own actions testify against you. And also. . ."

He nodded to her and, slowly, Evie stepped forward. She felt her wings tensing behind her, her legs bending slightly at the knee.

She threw off the hood that had shadowed her face. Then she pulled her lips back from her teeth and smiled.

She heard Molly's gasp of shock at seeing her, but she didn't turn her head. Her eyes were fastened on Troy.

He tried to back further away, but there was nowhere for him to go. Cold stone walls rose up on every side behind him. "Wait . . ." Troy moaned. "I can explain . . . just wait. . ."

The King ignored him. The King drew himself up to his full height, and his wings spread out so that they seemed to fill the whole cave. "Troy Bard," he said, letting the name roll slowly off his tongue. "Witnesses have given testimony against you as do your own, guilt-filled eyes. You must die."

Swiftly, they pounced.

One of the King's guards darted forward, kicking Troy's legs out from under him so that he fell heavily to his knees. Evie half-stepped, half-leaped through the air, her re-born body somehow knowing how to land gracefully beside Troy's cowering form. The guard wrapped one arm around his chest, pinning his arms to his side. Evie grabbed a fistful of his hair and pulled his head back, exposing his neck and forcing him to look up, into her eyes.

The King pulled a knife from his belt and held it out to her. In one smooth, swift movement, Evie brought the blade arching against the white of Troy's neck. His eyes bulged as knife kissed flesh. Red sprayed out, and Evie felt the strength fall from his limbs, watched the emptiness flood his eyes.

She threw back her head and trilled, a high-pitched cry of victory.

"Evie!" the King's voice thundered. "Restrain yourself! There are yet free-humans in this room!"

Evie's mouth snapped closed, and her eyes darted anxiously over to where Molly still crouched. But she had done no harm. Molly's eyes were filled with fear and caution . . . her mind was still her own.

Evie let Troy's body fall, limp to the ground. Slowly, afraid that Molly would pull away from her in horror, Evie moved closer, gently lowering herself down to Molly's side. Molly stared at her, her eyes wide with shock.

"Evie?" she whispered softly. "Is that really you?"

Evie nodded, but there was no way to explain things now. The King had turned to Molly. And his eyes were burning.

"You, too, must pay," his voice was filled with malice. Evie put a hand on Molly's shoulder, trying to comfort her. "You too would have done us the worst kind of harm," the King said. "You have broken our most sacred laws."

Evie brought her hands up to sign, desperate to convince the King to come to Molly's aid. But he shook his head at her, lifting a hand to wave her protests away.

"I didn't know." Molly's voice was low and halting. She kept glancing down at Jake, and Evie thought that she barely even knew what she was saying. "I didn't know what the cup was, or what it would do. But once we were here . . ." She shook her head at the memory. "I told Andrew to stop, but he wouldn't listen so I . . . I fought him."

"Please," Molly went on, her voice cracking. "Help me. Jake's still breathing . . . something could still be done. Please. . . he didn't do you any harm. He came here to protect me, not to break any of your rules. Help me to save him!"

"Why should we help you?" he demanded from Molly. "You came here and attacked our servants. You tried to steal something to which you have no right!"

"I *stopped* them from taking it!" Molly cried. "I took the cup from Andrew to keep him from using it! I gave it to that girl! Listen to my voice . . . you know my strength! She never could have forced it from me!"

"It is the strength of your voice that condemns you!" The King pointed at her as his voice climbed. "With a voice strong enough to defeat so many of our own, you could have thrown off your Holder's authority at any moment!"

"But I didn't know!" Molly shouted back. "Not until I came here, not until I defeated your guards! Look, we don't have time for this—he's losing too much blood." She gazed down at Jake's limp form in agony. "Please," she said, her voice soft for the first time. "I'll pay any price . . . do anything you ask."

Suddenly the King swooped down, crouching so that his eyes were level with hers.

"Swear it," he demanded, his eyes burning. "Swear that you will do me any service I desire."

Evie felt unease wash over her. Her fingers on Molly's shoulder tightened in silent warning. Without knowing why, she longed to cry out to Molly, to warn her to beware. But she could not speak a word. Molly glanced down once at Jake, and the words rolled smoothly off her lips.

"I swear," she said, looking the King in the eyes. "Anything. Anything at all. Just make him live."

"Done!" The King stood up swiftly, and Evie saw triumph in his eyes. Suddenly she knew that he had wanted to force just those words from Molly. Her vow would be a costly one.

"Quickly, now!" the King commanded, turning to the other Watchers. "We will take him to the Moon Pool."

BEA

Death had taken Bea by surprise one last time. It had been more patient than she imagined.

The pain had not stopped, but the worst of it had left her. She hardly even noticed the spasms when they shook her now. It seemed to her that she had floated for hours, staring up at a sky of perfect, unbroken blue. But perhaps it had been only minutes, after all.

"I knew you would come."

She smiled as Malachai circled her once in the air before lowering himself gently into the water beside her. He moved gingerly, trying not to rock her, or even touch her. She grimaced, knowing what he saw.

She felt it all, felt how one side of her face had collapsed into a gray, mottled ruin. Felt her body, already so paper thin, snap when brittle bones could not stand the way she thrashed when the pain was at its worst. Malachai wrapped his arms around her, gently, afraid to touch her. She nestled into his chest, moaning unabashedly as her skin touched his.

She looked up at the tears streaming down his face and reached a shaking hand to wipe them away. "Don't be sad," she rasped. "I was strong enough. I kept you safe." A smile played on her lips. "I would have . . ." She paused as pain surged and stole her breath for a moment. "I would have stayed with you, my love, if I could have. I would have stayed with you forever."

Malachai bent down and, with infinite care, pressed his lips gently to hers.

Bea pressed a hand to his cheek and held his face close to hers.

"Live," she said fiercely. "This isn't what we wanted . . . either of us. But I can . . . I can make my peace with it. If I know that you will keep trying to be happy. Trying to heal. Promise me?"

Malachai nodded and leaned in to kiss her again. Suddenly Bea stiffened in his arms, and she cried out, her voice raw and choked with agony. Malachai watched helplessly, holding her as her body convulsed. When it had passed, she looked up at him and smiled weakly.

"Will you sing me to sleep?" she asked.

Malachai shook his head frantically, but she knew he could not refuse her. "It's okay," she promised. "I've had enough. I don't want this anymore." She motioned weakly to her broken frame.

Malachai shuddered, and pulled her closer to him, bowing his head and squeezing his eyes shut. She knew that, for him, this was the real goodbye. The force of his voice would wipe away the woman he had loved. He leaned down and kissed her on the forehead one last time.

"My love will never leave you," Bea whispered.

Malachai looked down at her, his eyes full of tenderness. He cradled her cheek in his palm. He lowered his mouth close to her ear, and whispered with eyes shut: "I never wanted you to suffer for me. I would have suffered it myself if I could have. I would have suffered it a million times, to keep this pain from you. You are the whole world to me, and always will be. I love you so much, Beatrice."

He lifted his eyes and looked at her, but only happiness looked back at him.

Her eyes were empty, and she smiled up at Malachai with joy. All her pain had melted away; all memory of her suffering was gone. She smiled up at him, delighting in his closeness, nestling closer to his chest. Fresh tears coursed down Malachai's cheeks, and he threw back his head and sang.

He sang to her, and for her. He sang for himself, and for everything that they were losing. He rocked her in the water, cradled against his chest, and sang until long after her eyes had closed and her skin had lost its warmth. His song changed when he knew her soul had left him, but still, he sang until the sun sank into the water, and his song finally turned to sobs.

Then Bea's angel gathered her into his arms and flew away.

MOLLY

The ocean swept past below them, ancient and gorgeous and sapphire blue. The sun was setting. Orange and gold light refracted off the water like millions of sparkling jewels, and behind the cliffs stretched majestically up and to the sky.

Molly didn't care.

She didn't see it. The beauty, the splendor . . . it was lost on her; it meant nothing. All she saw was Jake.

A small cluster of the Watchers swarmed around him, flying awkwardly as they struggled to hold him aloft. Molly was hardly aware that she, too, was being carried through the air. Blood still leaked from Jake's wound. She could see the slow drip of red that fell and was then whisked away by the wind.

When they landed, Molly sprang forward, helping to support Jake's head as they lowered him to the ground.

She glanced over at the pool—the smooth water made milk-white by the mother-of-pearl stones that lay beneath it, its teardrop shape.

"What is it?" she asked as the King landed beside her.

"A gift from our mother," the King explained. "It allows us to heal ourselves from most injuries. Our wings are more delicate than they may seem to you . . . without it, most of us would be crippled and flightless by our thirteenth year."

"Will it save him?"

The King knelt down beside Jake's body and peered at him closely. Evie came and held Molly's hand, mutely offering what comfort she could.

"I cannot say. The pool can do much . . . but it cannot bring back one whose soul has fled. We must not wait."

The King nodded to two of the Watchers who stood nearby, and they quickly picked Jake up and placed him into the water. He sank quickly to the bottom.

"He won't be able to breathe!" Molly cried.

The King shook his head. "He does not need to breathe, as long as he is in the water."

The color of the water began to change, the whiteness of it mixing with the red that still bled from Jake's chest. A crust began to form over the surface, first like a light frost—then it thickened and grew, creaking slightly as it swelled up and over the water like a thick, white scab.

"What is that? What's happening?" Molly knelt by the side of the pool and reached out slowly. The King did not answer her, and the rest of the Watchers looked at her intently, silent. Her hands were shaking when she touched it . . . it looked like ice. But when Molly's fingers pressed against the shell, it was not cold. It was not ice, but salt. She pressed her face against the shell, trying to catch a glimpse of Jake beneath the surface, but the milky white color blotted everything out.

Molly did not know how long she knelt there. More Watchers came; she felt them arrayed behind her, observing silently. Evie stayed close by her side, and the King stood just a few feet away, gazing over at the ocean.

"He's an addict," Molly said suddenly, turning first to Evie and then to the King. "Can the water heal him of his addiction?"

The King looked down at her and shook his head, and his lips pressed into a hard line.

"The pool can knit together flesh, muscle, and tendon. Its power may suffice for that, and that alone. Be content."

Biting her lip, Molly nodded and turned back to the pool.

Thud.

Molly looked around her. Where was the sound coming from?

Thud.

"It's Jake!" she was screaming, beating her fists against the thick salt shell. She could just see his face. His eyes were open, and full of fear.

"He needs to get out. Oh God. Oh God! Someone get him out!"

Evie leaned forward and pressed one of her fingers against the shell. Her nail extended and grew into a sharp, curved claw. The ice shattered.

Molly reached down into the water, pulling on Jake's hand and dragging him up onto the ground beside her. He was whole and shaking, and Molly clutched him against her chest. It was then that the sobs came, deep and harsh and unashamed.

"I can't believe you're breathing," she gasped into his ear. "Are you really alright?"

"I think so," Jake whispered, his fingers stroking her hair. "It's alright. Look." He pulled away so that she could see his chest. Where the bullet had pierced him, there was now only a small circle of skin, shiny and smooth. Like a scar long healed.

"And look at my hand . . ." Jake held up his right hand, and Molly cried out in wordless wonder. It was perfect. The skin was smooth and un-scarred, as though flame had never touched it. Jake wiggled his fingers, wonder plain on his face. Molly brought his hand to her lips and kissed it gently.

"I don't know what I would have done . . ." she whispered, as the tears started again.

"I know," Jake answered, and he leaned in and kissed her. They kissed as though they were not surrounded by a crowd of strange, motionless creatures, as though they were alone in their little room, with nothing to fear.

"It pains me," the King interrupted, "but I must hold you to your oath."

Molly dropped her head to her chest and took a long, deep breath. Steeling herself, she pulled away from Jake and stood.

"I'm ready," she said.

Jake leaped to his feet. "Wait a minute. What oath?"

He pushed forward till he was standing between Molly and the King, shielding her from him.

"Whatever Molly promised you, she did it for me. For my sake. I'll take it on myself . . . I'll pay the debt."

The King smiled and shook his head. "Your heart does you credit, but we have healed you when no mortal power could have. You, too, are indebted to us."

Molly stepped forward so that she and Jake stood shoulder to shoulder. Her hand found his and their fingers intertwined.

"Alright," she said steadily. "What do you want from us?"

The King smiled and spread his hands in front of him apologetically. "I am afraid," he said, "everything."

EPILOGUE: MOLLY

"Are you sure about this?"

Two weeks later, the crowd in the Homeland bar buzzed all around them. Standing in front of the stage, Jake and Molly might as well have been in their own world.

"I'm sure." Molly slipped the jacket from her shoulders and laid it on the edge of the stage. "I get it now. I can keep it under control." She smiled at Jake, laying a hand against his cheek. "I can do this. I *need* to do this."

"I know you do." Jake reached up to take her hand, pressing it against his lips. He sighed. "Alright. It'll be fine. You go on up there and do your thing. Just try not to start a riot or anything, okay? We've had enough craziness."

Molly's smile tightened. "We have," she agreed. "But we're going to have a lot more. You know that, right? It'll get a lot worse before it gets better. If it ever does get better."

"Molly, listen." Jake leaned in close to her, lowering his voice, "Let's not worry about it. Let's not even think about what's coming. Right here, right now, we're together. I'm back in treatment. You're alive. That feels like a victory to me. It feels like enough."

"You're right." Molly smiled and glanced over her shoulder, to where Janice stood on stage, tapping her foot and watching them closely. "I'd better get up there. Wish me luck."

"Good luck," Jake muttered. "Try not to sing too well. Miss some notes. Forget the words every once in a while. Anything."

Molly laughed and bounded up to take her place at the microphone. Everything was just like she remembered. The warmth of the lights on her skin, the heavy smoke-smell of the air. The thrill of the audience's upturned faces. She took the mic in her hands and glanced around at the band. They had welcomed her back—of course they had. Only Janice seemed suspicious. She knew Molly too well and seemed to know that more was going on than Molly was willing to tell her. Molly smiled at Janice, trying to reassure her. But when Janice smiled back, she didn't quite meet Molly's eyes. She was studying Molly's neck, staring at the twin symbols that she and Jake now both wore, etched into their skin.

The music started, and the thrum of it was like electric current, traveling from Molly's eardrums straight to her heart. She felt it coursing through her, waking her up, watering the thirsty places in her soul that had begun to run dry. The tempo increased, and Molly felt her heart rate rise. She let herself forget. She forgot about Janice's anxious stares. Forgot about all that she had lost, about what she and Jake had endured. She forgot about the war that soon was coming. She looked at the audience, and at Jake, standing close in front of the stage. The worry had melted from his eyes, too. He smiled up at her.

The music swelled inside her. It felt different now, now that she knew herself well enough to hold back. It felt less explosive. But it was still beautiful and piercing and true, and it was still everything she wanted. Molly leaned in close to the microphone and closed her eyes.

She sang.

* * *

Molly's story begins in Magic Calls . . .

Don't miss the beginning of Molly's story . . .

Magic Calls

Available now on Amazon!!

http://www.miriamgreystone.com/getbook1

Want more? Check out Miriam Greystone's other urban fantasy series: The OUTCAST MAGE

http://www.miriamgreystone.com/TruthsightKindle

Meet Amy. Mage. Healer. Outcast.

Amy has a gift for healing supernatural creatures. But the one person she can't save is herself.

Forced to abandon her magic and live in hiding, Amy spends her days working in the ER and her nights running a secret clinic for supernatural creatures. But everything changes on the night that she comes to the aid of a centaur infant and its mother. When Amy's medical skills alone aren't enough to save their lives, she is forced to use her magic, revealing her identity to the mages who want her dead.

Fleeing for her life, Amy's only hope for survival may lie with a mysterious being named Rowan, who has a hidden agenda of his own.

Now Amy must join forces with the creatures who were once her patients and fight to uncover the one secret that may be powerful enough to save them all.

* * *

Did you enjoy this book? Reviews are vital to a book's success. Please consider leaving a brief review; even a few short lines will help this book find new readers. Thank you!

http://www.miriamgreystone.com/MagicCriesKindle

Be sure to join my Insiders list to get free sneak peeks, new release notices, and giveaways! Join here:
http://www.miriamgreystone.com/connect-with-me/

ACKNOWLEDGMENTS

This book goes to some hard places, and I want to thank the many people who have been in hard places, and gone through difficult times, by my side. My husband, whose love is a light for me in dark places. My children, who are the light of my life and give me more joy than can be described. My father, who is my teacher and also my friend. My sister, who puts up with me when no one else would, and has come through for me more times than I can count. My mother, whose absence is a constant source of pain, and whose memory is a constant source of comfort. Yocheved, whose friendship has been one of the anchors of my life. Kerry and Mike, who are two of the best people that I know—I feel so honored and lucky to call you family.

My critique partners, Grace and Michelle, who are also amazing friends and who are a huge part of bringing everything I write to life. Michelle Rascon, who once again did an amazing job of editing this book. Clarissa Yeo, who created one of the most beautiful covers I have ever seen.

And thank you again to all the readers. These stories are such a big part of me, and it means the world to me when others enjoy them and find them compelling. I am grateful that you read the books that I work so hard to create.

Love,

Miriam

ALSO BY MIRIAM GREYSTONE:

The Echoes Series

Magic Calls

Magic Cries

Magic Sings – *Coming soon!!*

The Outcast Mage Series

Truthsight

Winter's Mage

Printed in Great Britain
by Amazon